PURRFECT HIT
THE MYSTERIES OF MAX 48

NIC SAINT

PURRFECT HIT

The Mysteries of Max 48

Copyright © 2021 by Nic Saint

All rights reserved. No part of this book may be reproduced in any form by any electronic or mechanical means including photocopying, recording, or information storage and retrieval without permission in writing from the author.

This is a work of fiction. Names, characters, places, brands, media, and incidents are either the product of the author's imagination or are used fictitiously. The author acknowledges the trademarked status and trademark owners of various products referenced in this work of fiction, which have been used without permission. The publication/use of these trademarks is not authorized, associated with, or sponsored by the trademark owners.

Edited by Chereese Graves

www.nicsaint.com

Give feedback on the book at: info@nicsaint.com

facebook.com/nicsaintauthor
@nicsaintauthor

First Edition

Printed in the U.S.A

PURRFECT HIT

Time to Face the Music

As you probably know, cats are no mean singers. In fact we can probably compete with your most popular songbirds out there when it comes to belting out a tune. So when Odelia was tasked to write an article about Tab Fitch, the well-known pop star, it was no hardship to drive down to Fitchville, as the compound he built on the outskirts of Hampton Cove is called, and have a chat with the man. As it turns out, Tab might be popular with his fans, but he hadn't made himself popular with his neighbors, as evidenced by their relentless campaign against him. And that was even before a gruesome murder struck right at the heart of Fitchville…

CHAPTER 1

As you may or may not know, cats are creatures of habit. And for the longest time it has been my habit and Dooley's to spend part of the night in peaceful repose at the foot of our human's bed. But recently Odelia has started sleeping restlessly, tossing and turning and generally making a nuisance of herself and preventing us from getting any sleep.

According to her it's something to do with this minor experience she's going through called pregnancy, which is probably simply an excuse to create trouble for us, for how can something like a baby kicking away against her tummy and her body blowing up like a balloon cause her any kind of inconvenience? I am, of course, joking. I totally understand how sleep has become an elusive proposition for her, and therefore also for us.

And since Gran was away on holiday—she and her best friend Scarlett had signed up for a Norwegian cruise, thinking Norway is a tropical destination in the Caribbean while in actual fact it's probably one of your more frosty destinations you can pick out of the cruise vacation arsenal—

we'd been sleeping on Gran's empty bed for the past few nights.

Which, I'm going to be absolutely honest with you, also didn't feel right. A bed without a warm human body isn't exactly the same thing. So back to Odelia and Chase we'd gone, and probably a good thing, too, for cats are natural predictors for life-threatening emergencies, so if something should happen in the middle of the night to warrant a run to the nearby hospital, we'd be the ones in the know and responsible for raising the alarm.

Now I know that having a baby isn't anywhere near the same thing as having your house catch fire or an earthquake ravaging your home, but it is still a major event.

"I can't sleep, Max," said Dooley, my best friend and compatriot.

"Me neither," I said, casting a baleful eye on the source of the trouble.

Odelia had taken to occasional groaning and moaning in the middle of the night, and getting up at all hours to go to the bathroom. Something to do with the pressure the baby was putting on her bladder. And each time Chase would wake up, cast a worried glance at his beloved, then reluctantly put his head down again and try to go back to sleep.

"Do you think this is going to be our life from now on?" asked Dooley. "Being kept awake all the time?"

"I doubt it," I said. "Once the baby is born things are bound to settle down again."

"I have heard that babies make a lot of noise, though," he said. "And that they don't care whether they do it in the middle of the night or the middle of the afternoon. They're very inconsiderate that way."

"I'm sure Odelia's baby won't be like that. He or she will probably sleep all the time, just like we do, and won't be any trouble at all."

Dooley pondered these words, then decided to impart some more wisdom, as gleaned from one of the programs he likes to watch of an evening. "I've heard that babies can make the same noise as a jumbo jet. The racket is supposed to be deafening."

"Doubtful. No baby can make the sound of a jumbo jet. It's physically impossible."

"No, but it's true. They're so loud they have even invented special machines to muffle the sound. They're called baby monitors and people place them in the nursery and then make sure to close the door so the sound can't rupture their eardrums."

"You should really stop watching so much television, Dooley," I said. "It's starting to affect your common sense, if you ask me."

I'm usually not so hard on my friend, but lack of sleep has this effect on me: it makes me cranky.

And then when finally I had managed to doze off, Odelia's phone chimed and we all woke up with an annoyed groan.

"Who is it?" asked Chase sleepily as he rubbed his tired eyes.

"Dan," said Odelia, looking equally bleary-eyed. "Yes, Dan?" she spoke into the device. She listened for a few moments, then said, "All right, I'll be there," and hung up.

"What's wrong?" asked Chase.

"I don't know. Some emergency over at Fitchville."

"Fitchville? What's Fitchville?"

"It's what the locals have started calling the new compound Tab Fitch is building."

"The singer?"

"Yeah. He's been buying up houses and creating his own private village. Safe to say his neighbors aren't too happy. There's been plenty of animosity about this building frenzy."

"So what happened? One of his neighbors took a potshot at him or something?"

"No idea. All Dan said was that something happened at Fitchville and to get out there as soon as possible."

"Want me to join you? In case things heat up?"

"No, I'll be fine," she said as she managed to get up with some effort. "Probably just some minor thing that Dan has decided to make a big deal of. You know what he's like."

"Here, I'll help you," said Chase as he rounded the bed and steadied her.

But she playfully slapped his hand away. "I'm perfectly capable of getting in and out of bed under my own steam, thank you very much."

"I know, but still…" He gave her a look of concern. "Maybe you should sit this one out?"

"I'm pregnant, not on the precipice of death, babe. I'll be fine."

Chase didn't look entirely convinced, but then Odelia does seem to overestimate her capacity to navigate everyday life movements ever since she's doubled in size. I know I wouldn't mind a helping paw when I had to carry that much excess weight around. But seeing she wasn't going to budge, he reluctantly backed off and went about his business.

We arrived downstairs, well ahead of our humans, and found Harriet and Brutus giggling on the couch for some unfathomable reason. They were staring at something on Harriet's tablet—and when I say Harriet's tablet I'm actually referring to the tablet Odelia has given to all of us, but since Harriet has been using it the most, its ownership seems to have quietly transferred to her.

"What are you guys looking at?" asked Dooley curiously.

"Only the most interesting thing ever invented," said Harriet.

"The wheel?" I asked. "The printing press? The light bulb?"

"Astrology," said Harriet. "Did you know that you can predict just about anything by simply looking at your horoscope once a day? For instance mine says that today I don't have to bother leaving the house since I'll only run into all kinds of trouble. Which means I won't leave the house, since these horoscopes never lie. What about you, Brutus?"

"Mine says that today is a fine day for some vigorous physical exercise. Have to keep that old ticker ticking over."

"You better go for a nice long walk then, sweetie pie. You don't want to ignore what the stars have in store for you."

"What about me?" asked Dooley eagerly. "What do the stars say about me?"

"Just that you should keep quiet," said Harriet, a touch harshly, I thought.

"Oh," said Dooley. "You mean…"

"Be quiet, Dooley, there's a good cat. Now Max, on the other hand," said Harriet, "has to watch out for strangers you meet on the street. Especially when they offer you candy."

"Don't take candy from a stranger, Max," said Brutus warningly.

"I don't eat candy," I said. "And as far as I remember no stranger has ever offered me any either. So your advice is pointless, Harriet. Where are you getting this from anyway?"

"Madame Burnett. It's a new site but it's getting rave reviews on Google."

"Well, then it hast to be good, doesn't it? Because Google never lies."

"Just you wait and see, Max," said Harriet. "Madame Burnett is never wrong."

"Yeah, yesterday she predicted I was going to see light at the end of a long tunnel," said Brutus, "and when I got up to go to my litter box last night, I actually did see a light at the end of the corridor."

"That's the light Tex keeps burning so he doesn't tumble down the stairs when he gets up in the middle of the night," I said. "Though usually it's designed for kids, as anyone who's not Madame Burnett will tell you."

"Don't listen to him, tootsie roll," said Harriet. "Madame Burnett warns us about nasty skeptics, and clearly she was referring to Max."

Odelia was ready to head out, and now called for us to join her.

"Are you coming?" I asked.

"Haven't you heard a word I said?" said Harriet. "I can't leave the house today. Much too dangerous."

"And I need to get my morning exercise in," said Brutus.

"And I'm going to be quiet all day," Dooley murmured between closed lips.

And so shaking my head, I was off in Odelia's wake. Good thing I don't believe in all of that superstitious nonsense.

"Watch out for that candy, Max!" Harriet yelled after me. "Just say no!"

CHAPTER 2

I honestly didn't know what to expect. Mostly when we're called out to a place it's because some weird shenanigans have been going on, and more often than not dead bodies are involved. Today, though, no murders or other criminal activities had been reported. What had been reported was a cow that had accidentally stumbled into a pond. Though from the first report we got upon arrival, the 'accident' part was up for discussion.

"He did it on purpose!" the young man with the ginger whiskers cried as he stood gesticulating in the direction of a nearby farm. "He pushed her in just as I was taking my morning swim!"

The young man reportedly was a famous pop singer, who had made a name for himself in recent years as an up-and-coming celebrity. Apart from his ginger hair, said ginger whiskers and a sizable pair of glasses he looked a little funny, though for the life of me I couldn't really put my finger on it. Not at first, at least. But then I got it: he was pretty short, but his legs were even shorter, which caused the disconcerting effect.

"So what are we looking at here?" asked Odelia. "A man pushed a cow into your swimming pool?"

"It's not a pool," said the young singer. "It's a duck pond, which I occasionally use to take a morning bath in. It's very invigorating for the body, and excellent for the skin."

We took a glance at the pond, which didn't look like any duck pond I'd ever seen. For one thing, it didn't contain a single duck. It also had a small dock and a diving board, and didn't have the kind of green scum that can usually be found floating on pond surfaces. This one had pristine water, colored an unnatural blue, and I could clearly smell the chlorine. It even had steps so you could get in and out of the 'pond' without any hassle.

The only thing, in fact, that made this pool different from your regular garden-variety backyard pool was the sizable cow standing in the middle of it, gazing at us with the kind of vaguely interested look that is typical for cows the world over. As if to say: honestly, I don't see what all the fuss is about, y'all.

"And look!" the irate little man continued, turning around, and we all looked where he was pointing. And now I saw it: his backside was liberally smeared with a sort of greenish-brownish substance. And as I took a sniff, immediately I knew what that substance was: cow dung. And as our eyes followed Mr. Fitch's, they landed on a nice round piece of similar dung on the edge of the pool, where presumably the cow had done its business preparatory to diving udder-first into the singer's pool.

Someone had clearly stepped into the cow dung, detracting somewhat from its perfect round shape and jellied consistency. Though what it lacked in substance had found a new destination on Tab Fitch's erstwhile clean trunks, which now stank to high heaven.

"I slipped," Tab explained when Odelia eyed him with marked curiosity.

"Better tell me the whole story from the beginning," she suggested.

Tab took a deep breath, and said, "First thing when I wake up, I always go in for half an hour of yoga. It's my way of starting the day. And then, to cool off, I jump into my pond."

"Only it's not really a pond, is it, Mr. Fitch? It looks more like a pool to me."

"Well, it's a pond," he insisted, "not a pool."

"Because you didn't get permission for a pool so you decided to push for a pond instead?" asked Odelia, who, like any reporter worth her salt, had done her research.

"Do we really have to go into all that again?" the singer lamented. "It's not important, is it? What's important is that I was floating in my pond when all of a sudden I heard a mooing sound, and when I opened my eyes, found myself looking at this huge… beast! It was standing next to the pond, staring at me intently, and then before I could stop it, it simply jumped into the pool and joined me! I mean, it almost jumped on top of me! If I hadn't swum out of the way it would have crushed me and I would have drowned!"

"Was there anyone else around when the cow jumped into the pool?" asked Odelia.

"No, there wasn't," the singer had to admit.

"So your assertion that the cow was pushed…"

"She was pushed—I have no idea how he did it, but there was definitely pushing involved. When have you ever heard of a cow spontaneously deciding to go for a swim?"

"Maybe she likes you? Felt an instant attraction and wanted to join you in the pool?"

He gave Odelia a dirty look. "It's not funny, Mrs. Kingsley. As far as I'm concerned this is attempted murder by cow, and I want you to know that I'm pressing charges."

"So what happened after you left the pool?"

"The pond!" he said, and made to stomp his foot on the grassy edge of the pond, before thinking better of it, since we were right next to the cow dung, and a stomp would have made quite a splash at this point. "Of course I scrambled to get out of the pond, only I hadn't seen the little 'present' the cow had left, so I stepped in it and slipped and fell."

Odelia laughed at this, then quickly covered it by coughing into her fist. "Are you going to press charges for attempted murder by cow dung?"

"Ha ha, very funny." The little man crossed his arms and scowled at the cow. "How am I going to get this animal out of my pond is what I'd like to know. Not to mention the damage its hoofs must have caused. Probably trampled so hard in her panic at being shoved in that she kicked a hole in the floor, causing the water to start draining away."

"Chlorinated water and farmland don't go together well, sir," said Odelia. "You might be looking at some environmental charges yourself if word gets out about your... pond."

Now he turned his scowl on her. "I should have known that you'd simply come out here to mock me and to gloat at my misfortune." He wagged a reproachful finger in her direction. "Well, let me tell you one thing, missy. I'm the sole source of a lot of business coming this way, and a lot of new jobs. So you can laugh all you want, but the council loves me, and when I tell them what happened here today, Plontek won't know what hit him!"

And with these words, and a final withering glance at the cow, he stalked off, scratching his backside as he did, before remembering it was covered in muck.

"Where's that little fella going, then?" asked the cow now.

"Home, I guess," I said. "To freshen up."

"Pity. I was starting to like him. Funny little guy."

"What's your name, by the way?" I asked. "For the article,"

I clarified. "Important to get these details right and avoid rectifications and letters to the editor later on."

"Bella," said the cow. "Not very original, I know, but then Dunton isn't one for originality."

"That would be Dunton Plontek, your owner?" I asked.

"That's right. He's the one who told me to take a plunge this morning."

"And nudged you?"

"Oh, sure. Do you really think I'd jump into this here pool because I wanted to? I hate getting wet, cat, as I'm sure you of all creatures will understand."

"Oh, yes," I said, as I studied the water with a marked shiver.

"It's supposed to be invigorating," said Dooley. "Though I prefer to stay dry myself."

"So how did he get you to dive into this here pool?" I asked.

"He threw in my feed," said Bella. "All wet and chewy it was, too. Not very nice of him."

"He threw in your feed?" I asked, marveling at the ingenuity of this Mr. Plontek.

"Absolutely. Lay a trail all the way from the stable to here, and then once I was out here he took aim and threw in the rest. He also gave me a prod in the rear, which caused me to have that little accident that you see there. The little fella that was floating in the pool probably didn't notice, but then he wouldn't have, since Dunton made sure he couldn't be seen, lying flat on his belly as he did." She glanced idly in the direction of the farm, whose roof could be seen rising up behind some trees beyond. "He probably skedaddled it back the moment I landed in the pool with a big splash." She shook her head. "Nasty rotten trick he pulled on me. I hate it when my food gets all soggy. I like it fresh and crispy."

And as I related all this to Odelia, she smiled widely throughout the whole sordid tale.

"So now the big question is," said Bella, eyeing me sadly, "how am I going to get out of this mess?"

CHAPTER 3

Tab's wife Madison knew better than to laugh when she saw her husband storm into the house and up the stairs. He'd been locked into a fight with the neighbors for the past year, and while he'd managed to square almost all of them, Dunton Plontek proved the one most difficult to conciliate.

The Plonteks had owned the farm next door for generations, and weren't as easily encouraged by the promise of a big monetary reward as the other neighbors, who had at some point all accepted Tab's offer and sold their properties and moved away. And in so doing had made Tab's dream come true: to create his own small domain in the countryside, right on the outskirts of Hampton Cove, the town he'd grown up in and so had she, and live peacefully without being bothered by what the neighbors thought.

Now Tab could play his music as loud as he wanted, or throw parties all night long, or splash around in his pool without being seen or heard by anyone.

Except Dunton, who refused to sell, and had, by the looks

of things, managed to play a practical joke on her husband that morning, by infesting his pool with a bovine intruder.

"I'm going to take a shower," Tab muttered darkly before taking the stairs two at a time. She decided to follow him up, since she had some unfinished business to take care of. Some very important unfinished business, which she hoped to settle today.

And so it was with a spring in her step that she followed her husband into the bathroom. A spring, but also the fear that her hopes would be thwarted once again.

So she took out the device, assumed the position and hoped for the best.

Tab, meanwhile, was already in the walk-in shower, having divested himself of his soiled trunks, and deftly scrubbing away the last remnants of his cow encounter.

As she waited for the result to finally show, she had to still her beating heart, and a sudden sense of panic rushed through her, almost making her feel nauseous.

It had to work—it just had to. But when she finally screwed up the courage to look, she saw that once again… it hadn't.

She released a whimper of disappointment.

Tab, stepping out of the shower, caught sight of the pregnancy test. And when he saw the look on her face, immediately enveloped her into his arms. "Next time, babe," he said quietly, gently caressing her back. "We'll just keep on trying, won't we?"

She nodded wordlessly, not even bothered by the fact that he'd made her front all wet. And when he finally let go, she sank down on the toilet seat and studied the test for a few more minutes, as if by looking the result would change, then threw it in the trash can under the sink.

A knock at the door took her out of her reverie, and she was glad for it. She had a tendency to allow dark thoughts to envelop her and drag her down, and this week of all weeks she couldn't afford that kind of behavior.

They had guests, after all, and plenty of them.

Tab had just started recording his new album in his private recording studio, and so his producer was staying at the compound, and so were Tab's cousin, who was shooting a movie about the making of the record, and of course Tab's best friend since kindergarten, Saul Goff. With so many people and the responsibility of the new album, the atmosphere had been electric for days, even without cow-related incidents thrown into the mix.

"Have you had breakfast yet?" asked Tab as he towel-dried his hair.

She shook her head. "Just some fruit and yogurt."

"Have the others eaten?"

"Waiting for you, I think."

"Well, let's not keep them waiting. I want to get started as soon as possible." He glanced at her through the mirror. "Sunroom, you think? Or outside on the deck?"

"Outside is fine. It's a nice day for it."

The trouble with having multiple houses and locations is how to choose where to sit down for meals. It was a luxury, of course, but it still took some organizing. The bigger their property grew, the more maintenance, which is why they urgently needed to hire a manager to handle that part, and also a crew of people to keep things running smoothly.

She now became aware of how wet her shirt actually was, and walked out and into the bedroom to put on a dry one. She'd planned to head into town that morning, and leave Tab and the others to go about their business of laying down some new music tracks.

And she'd just changed into a fresh shirt when she overheard some harsh words being exchanged. The voices were drifting in from a nearby room. And as she listened, she recognized Saul's voice and Tab's, as they seemed to be in the throes of an argument.

It was rare for the two old friends to fight, but not surprising, considering the pressure Tab was under. The record company was expecting an album that would sell at least as well or preferably even better than the last one, which had been a number-one hit all around the world, spawning several big hits and turning Tab Fitch into a global star.

Numerous rewards, a sold-out tour, and all the craziness and attention that went with it had heaped on the pressure to prove he wasn't a one-hit wonder but an artist who was here to stay.

It had caused Tab a lot of sleepless nights over the past couple of months. Which is why Madison hadn't wanted to trouble him with her own problems. Even though he wanted to start a family as much as she did, he had other stuff on his mind right now.

She decided to slip out unseen, not wanting her husband or his best friend to know they'd been overheard, and soon was on her way into town.

And she'd already traveled a mile before she remembered she'd promised Tab they'd breakfast together—them and the rest of the crew.

Oh, well. She was sure they could manage without her.

CHAPTER 4

When Odelia takes on an assignment, she always tries to do a good job. So after our early-morning contretemps with Tab Fitch, she now took us in to see Julia Ulenberg, the woman in charge of the planning commission of our local town council.

In other words: the person who decides who can build what where in Hampton Cove.

She had agreed to see us in her wood-paneled office, which smelled of pine and honest sweat. Seated behind a large desk, Mrs. Ulenberg looked regal, like the ruler of her own domain, which I guess she was. She was dressed conservatively and if the cautious look on her face was anything to go by, wasn't a big fan of reporters, Odelia in particular.

"Clearly Mr. Fitch is making a mockery of our building laws," Odelia said, having placed her phone on Mrs. Ulenberg's desk to record the interview. "So why are you allowing him to buy up all of that land and those properties and operate his own private village?"

"I think you're exaggerating, Mrs. Kingsley," said the woman, eyeing the recording device with a baleful eye. "Mr.

Fitch isn't operating his own village. He's simply combining several of these properties into a larger one. And frankly I don't see the problem."

"The problem is that he's blocking off pathways, rerouting rural roads, making parts of Hampton Cove inaccessible to locals and generally creating his own personal fiefdom."

At this, the planning commission chairwoman had to laugh. "Fiefdom! Now there's a word I haven't heard in a while. You're painting Tab Fitch as some kind of feudal overlord, while in actual fact he's simply a very successful and extremely talented artist who's done very well for himself. In other words, a local boy made good. And in that sense a success story to be proud of and to be celebrated, not vilified." She gave Odelia a not-so-friendly look. "I know the press are always looking for a villain. A scapegoat. But I can assure you, Mrs. Kingsley, that there are no villains here, and no losers. Mr. Fitch deciding to take up residence in his hometown is going to prove a blessing for us, not a burden. It's going to attract tourists, and business, and provide favorable press—if we decide to embrace it."

"You have definitely embraced him, haven't you?" said Odelia, gesturing to a signed picture of Tab hanging on the wall. It read, 'To Julia, with all my heart—Tab.'

Mrs. Ulenberg shrugged. "So I'm a fan. I don't see what's wrong with that?"

"What's wrong with that is that it creates a suspicion of partiality on your part."

The woman stiffened. "I'm sure I have no idea what you mean."

"Dunton Plontek petitioned the commission to sanction Tab for taking a pond that was used by Mr. Plontek's livestock and turning it into a private pool. But his petition was summarily rejected."

"Tab owns the land that pond is located on, so Mr. Plontek's petition has no merit."

"He has a right of way, and his animals have had access to that pond for generations."

The woman now smiled. "I see you have been doing some research into the matter. But if you would have bothered to dig a little deeper you would have seen that Mr. Plontek's right of way has in no way been blocked. And as far as the pond is concerned..." She made a light shrugging gesture. "It's still there, isn't it? And if he wants, his cows can still make use of it. So I honestly don't see what the problem is."

"The problem is that it's not a pond but a chlorinated pool no cow will drink from."

"Except Bella, apparently," said Dooley.

I glanced over to my friend. "You have been noticeably quiet this morning," I said.

"Harriet's horoscope told me I should be quiet, so I've been trying to do as she said."

"You do know that these horoscopes are all made up, right? This Madame Burnett is just a freelance reporter paid to invent this stuff. So her predictions are appropriately vague—so vague they can literally mean anything—and people like it because it makes them feel that life is more predictable than it actually is."

"What are you saying, Max? That I shouldn't keep quiet all day?"

"That's exactly what I'm saying."

His face lit up with a look of relief. "Oh, phew! I was just thinking how difficult it is not to say anything to anyone all the time!"

"As far as I'm concerned you can say whatever you want to anyone you want whenever you want," I said, giving him a pat on the shoulder.

His face clouded again. "But... if what you're saying is

true, then maybe Brutus shouldn't exert himself—it could harm his ticker." He gasped in shock. "Brutus may die, Max! We have to do something... now!"

"I'm sure that a little bit of exercise won't hurt Brutus," I said.

He gave me a dubious look. "Are you sure?"

"Absolutely."

Mrs. Julia Ulenberg clearly had had enough of Odelia, for she now rose, and extended her hand. "I'm afraid I have to leave you now, Mrs. Kingsley. Important meeting. Can't wait. I trust you can see yourself out?"

And thusly dismissed, we left the office.

CHAPTER 5

For a moment, Odelia seemed irresolute. When you've got your mind set on cornering a person and getting some honest answers out of them, and then they simply dismiss you out of hand, practically showing you the door, the effect can be a little jarring.

"Okay, guys," she said. "Time to regroup."

"Maybe talk to the farmer?" I suggested. "I'm sure he'll have a few things to say about Tab Fitch and his pond-slash-pool."

"Good idea," said Odelia, pointing in my direction. "I probably should have done that first thing. Collect some more facts and material before trying to tackle this Ulenberg woman." She checked her watch. "First I need to be somewhere, though," she murmured.

"Hey there, cutie pie," suddenly a voice spoke in my rear. "Want a piece of candy?"

Both Dooley and I slowly looked up at the person. She was a blue-haired young woman who was holding out a piece of colorful candy in front of my nose. I took one sniff and found myself thinking that there was far too much sugar in the thing. My second thought was: what are the chances? And of course that's what Dooley latched on to.

"Madame Burnett was right! Run, Max, run!"

"I'm not running," I said. For one thing, I hate physical exertion, and for another, even though blue-haired, the woman didn't exactly look like a menace to society—or cats.

When it became obvious to her that I wasn't biting, she withdrew both her offer and her hand, and popped the piece of candy into her own mouth instead.

"Any idea where we might find Tab Fitch, miss?" she now addressed Odelia.

Next to her, a young man had materialized. Instead of offering us candy, though, he was offering us curious looks, as if he'd never seen a cat before in his life. "We know he lives around here," he explained. "We just don't know where, exactly."

"We're huge fans, you see," said the blue-haired girl. "Like, his biggest fans ever."

"Well, you more than me, Xanthe," said her companion.

"I met him once, you know," said Xanthe. "On tour? I go to all of his shows—or at least as many as I can afford. And he was playing this small venue in Delaware once, and I had won a backstage pass through our local radio station? And there were only five of us, and he shook our hands and talked to us for, like, an hour or something. It was so, so cool." Her eyes were sparkling, and I wondered what she would have made of Tab covered in cow dung. She probably would have thought it was so, so cool, even though it wasn't.

"We're on our honeymoon," the young man explained.

Xanthe held up her hand, displaying a ring. "Rasheed so didn't want to come. When I told him I wanted to go on a pilgrimage to Fitchville I swear I thought he was going to divorce me."

"I didn't," said Rasheed placidly.

"But you thought it."

"I really didn't."

"He's such a sweetheart," said Xanthe. "Imagine going to see some lame pop star on your honeymoon."

"I don't think Tab is lame. I'm just not as big a fan of him as you are, obviously."

"'Obviously,'" Xanthe mimicked him. She hooked her arm through her hubby's. "He's hilarious, isn't he? When I asked for Tab's latest hit as our first song at the wedding he didn't even complain. He just made this tiny eye roll when he thought I wasn't looking."

"I didn't roll my eyes."

"You did, too. You hate Tab, admit it."

"I don't hate Tab Fitch."

"You hate Tab but you love me, which is the only reason you're going along with this nonsense."

"I do not. I really don't."

Xanthe pressed a sweet kiss on the guy's cheek, then turned back to Odelia. "So any directions? This way? That way?"

Odelia smiled and explained to the young couple how to find the way to Fitchville.

"I'm going to take a selfie of you and me and Tab," Xanthe announced as they crossed the street.

"No, you're not."

"Oh, yes, I am."

We watched as they trotted off, then disappeared into an internet café.

"I didn't know they still existed," I told Odelia.

"What, fans?" she asked.

"No, internet cafés. Doesn't everyone have a smartphone these days?"

Odelia shrugged. "Maybe their battery died. Or they have one of those cheap cell phone plans with limited data." She frowned as she regarded us for a moment. "Are you sure you want to come? Cause you'll have to wait in the waiting room as Dr. Hoey doesn't allow pets in his exam room."

"Oh, absolutely," I said. Frankly after having had a front-row seat all through Odelia's pregnancy, I quite enjoyed these regular trips to the gynecologist. Even though we didn't get to go with her, we got to eavesdrop on the conversations of the women waiting along with us, and I have to say I'd never experienced a single moment of boredom.

"Do we have to?" asked Dooley, who's not all that keen on doctors—any doctors.

"No, like I said, you really don't have to come if you don't want to," said Odelia.

Dooley then glanced at me. "Do you want to go, Max?"

"Yes, I do," I said.

He sighed. "Then I guess I'll go, too. I really can't let Max out of my sight, you see," he explained. "Harriet's astrologer predicted that some dangerous people would offer him candy, and Max said it was all nonsense, but look what happened: dangerous people just offered him candy!"

"They didn't look all that dangerous to me," I said.

"She had blue hair!" Dooley cried. "It doesn't get more dangerous than that!"

I could have asked him how he'd formed that conclusion but frankly I didn't really want to know. Probably something to do with the hair dye affecting a person's brain.

And so it was that we entered the office of that all-important person in a pregnant person's life: the gynecologist.

And settled in for a long wait.

CHAPTER 6

"I don't understand," Dooley whispered.

"What don't you understand?" I whispered back.

For some reason a doctor's waiting room is particularly conducive to whispered conversations, even though nobody could understand us, of course.

"Odelia made an appointment, and still there are all these other people here. Have they also made an appointment at the same time as Odelia?"

"I think they're all ahead of her," I said.

"So we have to wait until the doctor has seen all of them?" he asked, aghast.

"I'm afraid so. Doctors are notoriously bad at time management. It's not something they teach in medical school, I guess."

But Odelia didn't seem to mind, or any of the other women. They were all leafing through the selection of magazines left on a small side table, or reading on their phones. One was even carrying out an equally whispered conversation with what could only be her mother, for she was saying, "No, I'm not going to divorce the no-good so-and-so!"

"But you should! He cheated on you WHILE YOU WERE PREGNANT!"

"I'm still pregnant," said the woman, darting nervous glances at the others, who were all working hard pretending not to listen intently to every single word she was saying.

"So get out while you have the chance!"

But then the door opened and a doctor's assistant called the woman's name and she hurriedly entered Dr. Hoey's inner sanctum.

Things did get a little boring after that, for no more conversation was forthcoming, all those present minding their own business and keeping themselves to themselves. The room slowly emptied out, and before long only Odelia was left, surfing the web and looking for more background information on Tab Fitch.

And she was just reading an article on Madison Fitch, Tab's young wife, when suddenly the lady in question walked in!

I glanced from the picture accompanying the article to the woman who'd entered, and I could tell that Odelia was doing the same thing. Now what were the odds? Slim to none, I would have imagined.

"You're Madison Fitch, aren't you?" said Odelia immediately.

Madison, who'd taken a seat, and was sporting sunglasses, immediately looked ill at ease. "Yes?" she said, as if fully expecting Odelia to ask her for a selfie. Or money. Or both.

"My name is Odelia Kingsley," said Odelia. "I was out at your place this morning, to talk to your husband about his pool incident—though I should probably say pond incident."

The woman relaxed a little. "Oh, so you're a police officer?"

"Reporter, actually. Though I do assist the police from time to time."

Immediately Madison was on guard again. "I really have no comment at this time," she said. "And if you want a reaction I'm afraid I'll have to refer you to my publicist."

"Oh, I don't want to interview you, if that's what you think," Odelia hastened to say. "Just that the chances of sharing the same gynecologist are probably very slim."

The woman smiled a stilted smile. "Yes, what are the odds?"

Not slim enough, in her opinion, that much was obvious.

Odelia is nothing if not a keen judge of character, and realizing that Madison Fitch was clearly ill at ease talking to a reporter about such a private matter as a visit to her gynecologist, she opted to keep her tongue, and both women lapsed into silence.

"She looks nice," said Dooley, studying the famous pop singer's wife. "And pretty."

"As long as she doesn't offer me any candy, I can only agree with you," I quipped.

Dooley's eyes went a little wider as he now carefully examined the woman's hands. But when he saw that she wasn't bearing gifts in the form of candy, he quickly relaxed.

"I see you brought your cats," said Madison now, and the sound of her voice must have caught Odelia by surprise, for she started a little.

"They are yours?" Madison asked.

"Yes, they're mine," said Odelia. "The orange one is called Max, and the gray one is Dooley. Though I should probably say blorange," she quickly amended her words. "Max is very particular about the color of his fur."

Madison gave Odelia a strange look, but seemed to have determined that Odelia wasn't a paparazzo or one of those reporters who enjoy badgering celebrities or their wives. "I love cats, but unfortunately Tab is allergic, so we can't have any."

"Soon you'll have your own sweetheart from the looks of things," said Odelia, gesturing to Madison's belly, which was as flat as a pancake.

Madison's smile faltered and I could tell that her guard immediately went back up. "Yes. Yes, of course," she said automatically. "And how about you? You look ready to burst."

"Only a couple more weeks," said Odelia. "If it were up to my husband he'd lock me up at home and not allow me to leave until it's time to take me to the hospital. But I like to keep busy, you know. And as long as I can, and I feel comfortable, why not?"

"What does he do, your husband?"

"Oh, he's a police detective."

"Well, let's hope he doesn't put you under arrest," said Madison.

Odelia laughed at this. "When I wake up one of these days, handcuffed to the bed, I'll remember that."

"Stop staring at the woman's handbag, Dooley," I whispered.

"I'll stop staring when I'm absolutely sure she doesn't have any candy in there!" my friend whispered back, and resumed his vigilance.

※

Madison was navigating the short drive from Hampton Cove to Fitchville, as the locals had started calling the compound. Even Tab liked the name, and had been giving it a spin lately, and even suggesting that they put up a sign at the entrance, 'Welcome to Fitchville.' Of course he would like that. Any man would, as the ultimate stroke to his ego. Then again, she had to admit she loved the place just as much as he did. They'd both grown up in Hampton Cove, and had always talked about moving back one day, and now that they had, neither of them had regretted it for a single moment. It just felt like home.

She thought back to her visit to the gynecologist. He was frankly puzzled that she was having such a hard time conceiving. All of her tests had come back positive, and the only thing he could think was that she was under a great deal of stress, which might affect her in an adverse way. Tab's tests had also been fine. Excellent volume. Great motility.

As she turned a corner, she almost hit a man coming from the other direction. She immediately recognized him as Dunton Plontek. The ruddy-faced farmer was dressed in his usual dirty blue coveralls and wearing his customary frown. He was walking in the middle of the road, as if daring any driver to run him over, which she almost had.

But instead of jumping out of the way, he simply kept on walking, giving her a hard stare as he went past. She had to maneuver the Range Rover all the way to the side of the road to let him pass, and if not for some deft steering on her part would have hit the ditch.

She watched him walk off in her rearview mirror and wondered not for the first time what would make the stubborn man finally yield. Or even if he'd eventually yield.

She righted the car and navigated the remainder of her journey at a more sedate pace, careful to brake before hitting any bends in the road. The last thing they needed was for her to run down one of the locals. Or even one of Dunton's cows.

She parked her car in the garage, neatly squeezing in between Tab's red Lamborghini Aventador and his newly acquired Ferrari Enzo, and got out. And as she crossed the gravel drive between the garage and the main house, she saw Darnell slam the door and walk off.

She held up her hand to wave at Tab's cousin, but he was

staring at the ground as if it had personally offended him, and clearly had no inkling he was being watched. His face was a thunderstorm and she wondered what was going on.

Darnell was in charge of filming the entire process of how Tab's new album was made, from conception to taping to the global tour that would follow in the spring. Tab had struck a lucrative deal with Netflix and the movie was already being touted as the most important musical documentary since Martin Scorsese's *Shine a Light* about the Rolling Stones. Darnell had full access to his cousin, and since they'd known each other since they were born—they were the same age—it promised to be a rare look into the life of the artist.

Madison watched Darnell round the corner of the house and then walked in.

Whatever was going on between her husband and his cousin was probably due to those age-old creative differences.

Definitely nothing to concern herself with.

CHAPTER 7

We were finally back in Odelia's office, and I could tell that Dooley was glad for this respite. At least here no one could offer me any sweets and lure me away to certain death. Though you never know, of course: someone might drop by with a bag full of the stuff.

Sometimes I find it hard to imagine what it must be like to be Dooley, with danger around every corner. So I was glad when he slipped into a peaceful slumber, even though he was kicking out with his hind legs from time to time, in the throes of a bad dream.

Odelia was busily typing away at her laptop, working on her article on that morning's skirmish between Tab Fitch and Bella, and she now turned her laptop to me. "What do you think, Max?" she said, and I smiled when I saw the picture she'd surreptitiously snapped of Tab's behind covered in cow dung.

"Front-page stuff," I told her, and we both laughed heartily.

"I'd love to see Tab's face when he sees this," she said with a happy grin.

"Did you take a picture of Bella, too?" I asked

She clicked through a couple of the snaps she'd taken and showed me a particularly nice one of Bella, standing in that pool and looking into the camera with perfect equanimity.

"A born photo model," I said. "You should go the whole hog and organize a shoot."

"Not sure what her owner would say. If Dunton Plontek really is this ornery guy Tab is making him out to be, he'll probably tell me to take a hike."

"Have you set up an interview with him yet?"

"I've been trying to get in touch, but he's a hard man to reach."

"Too busy luring cows into his neighbors' ponds."

"You have to admire the gall of the man," said Odelia, but before she could say more, suddenly the door to the outer office opened and closed and moments later not Plontek strode in, but Chase. And judging from the grave expression on his face he wasn't happy.

"What's wrong?" asked Odelia immediately.

"It's Tab Fitch," said the burly cop. "He's been murdered."

🐾

We were en route to Fitchville, with Chase relaying the little bit of information he was in possession of, as received by Dolores Peltz, our local 911 dispatcher.

"Fitch's wife called it in."

"Madison," said Odelia.

"Said she arrived home and found him in his studio, which apparently is located underground, halfway between the house and a bar Fitch opened on the premises. She tried to revive him, but quickly saw it was no use, so she called an ambulance."

"It's so hard to believe," said Odelia. "I just talked to him this morning."

"About the cow incident," said Chase wryly.

"Yeah."

"Do you think this farmer—this Dunton Plontek could be involved?"

"I don't know. There's a big difference between dunking a cow into a person's pool and murdering them. How did he die? Did Madison say?"

"No idea. According to Dolores she sounded very panicky on the phone."

"Of course she did. Imagine coming home and finding your husband like that." She darted a quick look at Chase, apparently to make sure he was still breathing.

"It was the candyman, Odelia," said Dooley, scooting forward. "He did it."

"The candyman?" asked Odelia. "You mean like in the movie?"

"I don't know about a movie, but it was definitely him. Or her." He frowned for a moment. "That woman with the blue hair, the one who tried to lure Max with candy, she wanted to pay a visit to Mr. Fitch, didn't she?"

"Yeah, she's a big fan, apparently. A self-confessed groupie."

"Look no further," said Dooley decidedly. "She did it. She's the candyman."

"Candy girl," I corrected my friend.

"She killed him with candy."

"How can you kill a person with candy?" asked Odelia.

"What are you talking about?" asked Chase.

"Dooley thinks this groupie I met this morning did it. He thinks she killed him with candy, so I was curious to know how you can kill a person with candy."

"Maybe by stuffing it down their throat so they choke?" Chase suggested.

"Great thinking, Chase!" said Dooley. "Case solved!"

"That was quick," said Odelia, producing a smile in spite of the circumstances.

We soon arrived at Tab's compound, and for a moment it wasn't entirely clear where we should be going. But then a sign that said 'Visitors This Way' directed us to a circular drive located behind what I assumed was the main house, and we all got out.

An ambulance was already parked there, and also three more police cars.

Madison Fitch was waiting for us, clutching a distraught hand to her throat. Next to her a man stood who reminded me of Tab himself: bespectacled and red-haired. But contrary to Tab this man was tall and gangly.

"Hi again," said Madison, who looked teary and fragile, then offered Odelia a weak smile. "Oh, this is Tab's cousin Darnell Fitch."

"The others are all downstairs," said Darnell. "We'll take you there."

"You won't find it on your own," Madison explained. "The studio is right underneath our feet."

Dooley glanced down at the blond gravel, as if expecting it to open up and swallow us. "Better ask them about the groupie," he now suggested. "Arrest her before she escapes."

"Later," I told him. "Let's find out what we're dealing with first."

As Madison and Darnell took us into the house, she explained, "I'd just got back and went looking for Tab to tell him about my visit to…" She glanced over to Odelia, who nodded. "So I called him on his mobile, but he didn't pick up, which I didn't think anything of at the time, since he's always so busy, and especially now, with the new album."

"I've been filming the whole process," said Darnell, "and the last time I'd seen him was in the studio. I'd popped out to get some fresh air—being cooped up down there can start to feel a little claustrophobic sometimes—and when I got back I bumped into Madison. So I told her Tab was working in his studio, and we went down to look for him together."

"And that's when we found him," said Madison. "He was on his back, looking pale… I thought he'd fainted. He often skips breakfast when he's working, even though I've told him he shouldn't. But when we came closer, I saw that…" Her voice faltered.

"There was something on his neck," said Darnell. "Some red mark or something, and when I felt for a pulse, there wasn't one. So Madison started doing CPR."

"It didn't work," she said quietly.

We'd gone down two flights of stairs and were now walking along a narrow corridor, with long LED tubes providing an eerie bright light. Soon we arrived at a sturdy-looking door, and Madison pushed it open. On the other side was a large space, with a low wooden ceiling, carpet on the floor and plenty of instruments and musical equipment spread throughout: a piano, several guitars, a violin, synthesizers, a drumkit…

"This is where he rehearses," said Darnell. "The actual studio is further down that way."

We passed through another door, and found ourselves standing in a soundproof studio, with the recording booth on the other side of a thick pane of glass.

Bent over the inert body of Tab Fitch was Abe Cornwall, the county coroner, while a small army of crime scene personnel were examining the scene.

"Dead," Abe determined when he caught sight of us.

"You better leave us now," Chase told Madison and Darnell. "But please don't go far. We'll want to talk to you."

Madison nodded, and even though Darnell seemed reluctant to follow Chase's instructions, he still complied. There was a strange expression in the young man's eyes. As if he was more angry than mournful over the death of his famous cousin.

The door swung closed again with a sort of swooshing sound, and then Chase turned to the coroner. "What can you tell us, Abe?"

"Garroted, from the looks of things. But since the actual garrote has been removed from the scene, it's hard to know what to look for. Thin piece of wire is my best guess."

"Like a guitar string?" Chase suggested, gesturing to a guitar lying next to the singer.

"Yes, that would do very nicely," said Abe. He picked up the guitar with gloved hands and studied it more closely. "I'm not an expert, but aren't there usually six strings on these things?" He flicked a loose-hanging piece of string at the head of the guitar, as if it had recently snapped—or been cut by someone with murder in mind. "Better wrap this up and take it along with us," he told one of his assistants, and handed them the guitar.

"Time of death?" asked Chase, who'd crouched down next to the body and was subjecting the wound to a closer scrutiny.

"Not that long ago," said Abe. "Body is still warm, so I'd say he died not long before he was found, which was, what, an hour ago? So let's say between one and two hours."

Odelia checked her phone. "Which would put time of death between twelve and one."

"I can live with that," said Abe with a courteous smile in Odelia's direction. "So not much longer now, huh? Are you sure you want to be gallivanting around dead bodies, honey?"

"I'm fine, Abe," said Odelia, giving the man a warm smile.

"At least if something happens you have a doctor on

hand," said Abe with a glance to Chase, who was doing his best to pretend he was fine with his wife assisting him at this time. As Odelia had indicated that morning, he wouldn't have minded if she took a leaf from Harriet's page and stayed home altogether.

"So you talked to him this morning?" said Abe.

"Yeah, I interviewed him after he found a cow in his pool."

"A cow in his pool! How did that happen?"

"A neighboring farmer managed to lure the animal into the pool by dumping some feed in. He and Tab have been locked into a conflict for weeks, apparently."

"We better have a little chat with that farmer," said Chase.

As we left, we came upon Madison, who'd been patiently waiting in the rehearsal space. Of Darnell there was no trace. Tab's wife had been pacing the room and now walked up to us. "I forgot to mention this earlier, but when I arrived back from my trip into town, I almost ran down Dunton Plontek. He was coming from the direction of the house, walking in the middle of the road. I almost drove my car into a ditch trying to avoid hitting him. He looked very angry, but then I guess he always looks very angry."

"What time was this?" asked Chase.

"Must have been... around twelve, maybe? I didn't really pay attention. Oh, and one other thing..." She glanced nervously to the door. "When I arrived, I saw Darnell coming out of the house. He looked upset for some reason. No idea why. And this morning, when I was getting ready, I overheard my husband arguing with Saul."

"Saul?"

"Saul Goff. He's Tab's best friend. They've known each other since they were kids. I just thought you'd want to know."

"What were they arguing about?"

"I couldn't hear. I just heard raised voices coming from

one of the rooms, and I recognized them as Tab and Saul. But I wasn't close enough to hear what they were saying." She gave them a worried look. "It's probably nothing, but the officer I talked to before told me to try and remember anything unusual that happened this morning, and to tell you as soon as you arrived. So I've been going over everything in my head, and those things stood out for some reason."

"You're doing fine, Madison," said Odelia.

"Are you here… as a reporter?" asked Madison now.

"No, I'm here as a police consultant now."

The woman nodded. She looked slower on the uptake somehow, as if what happened hadn't fully registered yet. The shock from finding her husband dead, of course. Everyone responds differently, and sometimes the reaction is delayed. I had the impression that that was what we were seeing here. Soon now, within the next few hours or days, it would hit her. I just hoped that there would be someone there with her when it happened.

Odelia must have been thinking along the same lines, for she now said, "Is there someone who can be with you right now, Madison?"

She stared at Odelia for a moment, then finally snapped out of it, blinked and nodded. "Yes. Yes, my parents said they'd be here any moment now. They're going to stay here with me for a while. And of course Saul is here, and Darnell, and Val."

"Val?" asked Chase. "Who's Val?"

"Val Kip. He's Tab's producer." She glanced around distractedly. "He should be here, actually. Tab was supposed to work with him on the new record all morning. I can't imagine where he could have gone off to."

"The candy girl," said Dooley knowingly. "She's more cunning than we thought, Max. She must have killed them all!"

CHAPTER 8

Madison had been so gracious to hand us a laminated map of Fitchville, though of course she didn't call it that. It contained several properties, with paths connecting them, and even an actual bar where people could go and have a drink—though it was reserved for Tab and Madison and their guests. There was also an underground cinema, next to the recording studio, a pizza parlor, an Olympic-size pool, helicopter landing pad, tennis court, mini-golf course…

We found the cousin, Darnell Fitch, smoking a cigarette in the meeting area in front of the orangery. It was obscured by an arc of cherry trees. He was staring before him, taking long drags from his cigarette. He appeared startled when we approached.

"I'm sorry I bailed on you back there," he said when Odelia and Chase took a seat. "Finding Tab like that… it just… shook me, you know. He was like my brother and my best friend. To think that he's gone… I just can't seem to take it in. He was such a force of nature." He took another long drag from his smoke and blew out a plume.

"I'm afraid we need to ask you a few questions, sir," said Chase now.

"Of course. What do you want to know?"

"You're staying here at the compound in an official capacity?"

"Yes, Tab signed a Netflix deal last year to document the making of his new album. But it's going to be much more than that. I've been filming my cousin for years, long before he ever made his first record, following him around everywhere—from the very first time he performed live in front of an audience—at a school dance when he was sixteen—to the first EP he recorded... I was right there next to him from the very beginning. Not as a videographer, of course. I was just an amateur in those early years, just like him, but more as a couple of friends goofing around. But now that footage has suddenly gained a lot of importance, with his career taking off into the stratosphere, and we were planning to put a selection of it in the Netflix film. Sort of a making of the new album, combined with an overview of his career up to this point, and then culminating with the new tour."

"So you're like your cousin's official chronicler," said Odelia with a smile.

"Yeah, something like that. It's been a wild ride, I can tell you that. We've been all over the world together, and now for it to end like this... It's just... I mean, it's just terrible."

"Around the time your cousin died you were seen leaving the house," said Chase. "Can you tell us where you were going?"

Darnell frowned. "When was this?"

"Twelve. The person who saw you said you didn't look happy."

The frown deepened. "I'm not sure..." Then he brightened. "Oh, that's right. Tab had just started rehearsals and I didn't feel like I was really needed down there in the bunker, as he liked to call it, so I decided to go for a walk. Get some fresh air, you know."

"You didn't get into an argument with your cousin?"

"Oh, absolutely not. Tab and I were like brothers."

"Brothers argue. And those arguments sometimes turn pretty nasty."

"Not Tab and me. We got on really well. In general Tab wasn't one to get into fights with people. He was a very laid-back kind of guy."

"So is there any reason why you would have looked so unhappy when you went for your walk?"

The man stared at Chase for a moment. "I… well, I've been under a great deal of pressure lately. Netflix wanted to push the release date for the documentary forward by a couple of weeks, and I still have a ton of editing to do to whip the material into shape. So what your witness perceived as me looking unhappy was probably just me looking stressed." He mashed out the stub of his cigarette. "Which is probably the reason I took up smoking again. I quit three years ago, but one month into landing the deal and I'm suddenly chain-smoking and so was Tab. Bad habit, I know, but it seems to go with the territory."

"Can you think of anyone who would have held a grudge against your cousin, Darnell?" asked Odelia, adopting a more conciliatory tone than Chase had been using so far. "Anyone who would have meant him harm? Or someone he got into conflict with recently?"

Darnell shook his head slowly, even as he shook another smoke from a pack. "Well, there's Steve, of course. Steve Rovira."

"Who's he?" asked Chase, jotting down the name on his notepad.

"Tab's old producer. Steve produced Tab's first two albums, the second of which was his big breakthrough.

Reached number one and stayed there for weeks. Won plenty of awards and broke all kinds of records. But then at some point, while they were starting to prepare to get back into the studio, Steve and Tab fell out over some royalties business."

"Royalties business?"

"Yeah, according to Steve, Tab had promised him a shared songwriting credit on the music from his first two albums, since they collaborated so closely together while they were making them, only when push came to shove, Tab decided not to honor that verbal agreement."

Chase whistled through his teeth. "Cutting Steve out of a lot of money, I assume?"

"Millions," said Darnell curtly. "Steve wasn't happy about it. It led to them severing all ties, Steve lawyering up, and Tab opting to hire a different producer for the new album."

"Who's the new producer?"

"That would be Val Kip."

"Who was supposed to be in the studio this morning," said Chase, nodding, "but is nowhere to be found."

"Probably in his room upstairs," said Darnell with a shrug.

"Any idea where this Steve Rovira is right now?"

"He's in town, actually," said Darnell. "I bumped into him the other day. Said he was staying at the Star. Said his lawyers are in the process of setting up a meeting with Tab's lawyers, with himself and Tab also present at the meeting. Though Tab was kicking up a big fuss. Refusing to go anywhere near Steve. Said it hampered his creative process."

"Is that a fact," said Chase quietly, directing a keen look at Odelia.

CHAPTER 9

As Odelia and Chase tried to settle on a plan of campaign of who to talk to next, we bumped into Madison, who said she'd seen Saul Goff in The Tab, the bar Tab had built for his friends. And since I think we were all curious to know what Saul and Tab had been arguing about that morning, we set foot in that direction.

"I'm worried, Max," said Dooley, giving me a worried look.

"Worried about what?" I asked, wondering if The Tab would serve kibble. Most bars are geared toward humans, of course, but some also keep some pet food in store. I hoped that Tab's The Tab was that kind of bar.

"Worried that we still haven't been able to track down Xanthe and Rasheed. They're the ones who killed Tab, and who knows what they're up to next. Nothing good, I think."

"We'll get around to them," I promised my friend. "Though for all we know they never got here."

"They looked pretty determined to talk to Tab and get their selfie—or more."

I decided to leave the jumping to conclusions to Dooley. I

prefer to deal in facts, you see, and this kind of idle speculation has never served any detective worth his salt.

Saul Goff was indeed sitting at the bar, hoisting a rather large pint of beer to his lips, and judging from the unfocused look in his eyes, it wasn't his first one either, a fact confirmed by the barman who held up ten fingers and then shook his head in dismay. Presumably The Tab was that rare bar where the guests didn't have to pay, the tab being picked up by Tab, which might not be as good an idea as it seemed on the surface.

"Saul Goff?" asked Chase as he placed a hand on the man's shoulder.

Saul blinked and looked up uncertainly. "Speaking," he said as he tried to focus on the big man standing next to him. "And who are you?"

"Chase Kingsley," said Chase, producing his police badge. "Hampton Cove Police Department. And this is Odelia Kingsley, police consultant."

"Kingsley and Kingsley?" asked Saul. "Are you two a double act, then?"

"Married, actually," said Chase.

"Oh," said Saul, as he gave this some thought. He was a sinewy man with fair hair, eyebrows so faint they were almost non-existent and big blue eyes that were a little watery after all the free alcohol he'd imbibed. "So... are you here to arrest me, officer? Only I haven't done anything... I don't think. I haven't even stepped into my car yet."

"And I definitely hope you're not going to. Not in this condition, at least."

"Oh, no, sir. I live here, see? So I'm not going anywhere."

"That's fine, Saul. How long have you been here?" He directed a quizzical look at the bartender, who was polishing glasses with a towel.

"All morning," the bartender mouthed, then rolled his eyes.

"I've been here... ever since we got back," said Saul uncertainly. "We were in the Bahamas, you see, writing songs? And then we came back here to record them."

"You and Tab wrote songs together?" asked Odelia.

"Oh, no. I'm not a songwriter. I wouldn't know where to begin. No, that's all Tab. He's the talent, I'm just there to make sure he's able to work in peace. I'm his fixer, see?"

Chase nodded, then adopted a more gentle tone. "Has anyone told you about what happened to Tab, Saul?"

That confused look was back. "What happened to Tab? What do you mean?"

"I'm afraid we have some bad news for you, Saul," said Odelia.

The man was just gaping now, his eyes shifting from Chase to Odelia. "Bad... news?"

"I'm afraid that Tab is dead, Saul," said Chase.

There was a sort of gulping sound, which came from the bartender, who must have realized that his days of dispensing free drinks to his employer's friends were over, and then a strangled little cry that escaped Saul's throat.

"Dead?" he finally asked, sounding like a child who's just discovered that Santa isn't coming this year. "What do you mean, dead?"

"We found his body in his recording studio just now. Looks like foul play."

"Foul play? You mean he was... murdered?"

Chase nodded.

"But... that's not possible. That can't be."

"I'm sorry to say that it is."

"But... who-who-who would do such a th-th-thing?"

"That's what we're trying to find out, Saul."

"And that's why we need your help," Odelia added.

The man turned to face the front again. "Tab… dead," he muttered, his eyes turning misty.

"Can you think of anyone who would want to harm Tab?" asked Chase.

Saul was shaking his head disconsolately. "No one. Tab is the salt of the earth. Best friend I ever had. Through thick and thin. More like a brother to me than my own brother."

"What exactly did you do for Tab, Saul?" asked Odelia, placing a comforting hand on the man's shoulder. Somehow Saul reminded me of a dog. The faithful kind, I mean, not the mean-spirited yapper. More like the dog that followed Richard Gere around everywhere in that movie, even after Richard wasn't amongst the living anymore.

"I did everything for Tab," said Saul quietly as a big tear leaked from his eye and fell into his beer. "I cooked for him, I washed his clothes, drove his car, flew his helicopter, worked as his main roadie when he was on tour, provided security, cleaned him up when he had too much to drink, got him his medicine… I was like his body man. His guy."

"Can you think of anyone who'd want to cause him harm?" Chase repeated.

"All I can think of is a crazed fan," said Saul after giving this some more thought. "Like John Lennon? You wouldn't believe how many nuts are out there. All wanting a piece of him. If you'd let them they'd rip him to shreds if they could, just to get their hands on a sock, his underpants, a lock of hair. It's scary what these so-called fans are capable of."

"See, Max?" said Dooley, giving me a bright-eyed look. "It's the groupies—I told you!"

"Let's just wait and see," I said, not wanting to get ahead of ourselves here.

"Oh, and of course there's that nutso neighbor," said Saul. "He kept giving us grief."

"Dunton Plontek?" asked Chase.

"That's the one. Can you believe he put a cow in Tab's pool this morning? Pity I wasn't there, or I would have given the guy a piece of my mind. You'd think you'd feel safe in your own pool, wouldn't you? But the guy was always pulling stunts like that. Determined to make our lives miserable. Obviously unhinged, if you ask me. I mean a cow? Really?"

"You and Tab were overheard arguing this morning," said Chase. "Can you tell us what that was about?"

"Arguing? Me and Tab? Impossible. Tab and I never fought. I told you, the guy was like a brother to me."

"Madison overheard the two of you," said Odelia. "It sounded serious."

"She must have misheard. Probably someone else having a go at Tab."

"Like who?"

"Like… well, I don't know, but it definitely wasn't me. I loved him. I loved him so much!" He burst into tears for real, and we decided it was best to leave him be for now.

CHAPTER 10

We were finally set to meet the infamous Dunton Plontek. And I must say I was curious to see what kind of person would use a cow to intimidate a person. It was safe to say that Mr. Plontek's dwelling was a lot less glamorous than that of his famous neighbor. The farmhouse itself was in need of some serious repair: especially the roof had seen better days and actually had a small tree growing through it, with several tiles dislodged and having gone walkabout. The chimney stack had taken a hit and the weather vane was stuck at an odd angle, certainly no longer capable of pointing out which direction the wind was blowing from. But then perhaps the same could be said for the farmer who inhabited the dilapidated structure. Unhinged? Possibly. Determined? Definitely.

"Dead," the man growled. "Are you sure?"

"I'm afraid so," said Odelia.

"Well, that's too bad," said the man, much to our surprise. He seemed to ponder the fate of his neighbor for a moment, then shrugged a pair of bony shoulders. "That's life."

Dunton Plontek was a large, angular man. His face

seemed to consist of plenty of bones jutting out at strange angles, and so did his body, as if nature had been in possession of enough bones to fit into one-and-a-half person and had decided to use them all on him. Even his ears stuck out, and I do realize ears aren't bones, but they did seem to fit in with the rest of him.

"You were seen leaving Tab's compound around twelve," said Chase. "Any reason?"

"Just taking a look at what the guy was up to this time," Dunton grunted. "He was always building stuff, you see. You'd wake up one morning and another new eyesore had suddenly popped up. Had to keep a close eye on him. Next thing you know he would have built a replica of the Eiffel Tower or the Statue of Liberty, scaring my cows off their milk."

"Did you enter the house at any point?"

"Nope. He would have kicked me out, wouldn't he? Kept as close an eye on me as I kept on him. Told his goons not to allow me anywhere near his property. People like him think they can just come here and take over. Build an entire village right next door. Soon he'd have his rock concerts here, with people trampling all over the place, parking their cars on my land, destroying the grass and turning the whole place into a garbage dump."

"Is that why you put a cow in his pond this morning?" asked Odelia. "To send him a message?"

"That was no pond," said the farmer, and spat a wad of some brown substance on the ground. "It used to be a pond, but he turned it into a swimming pool. And the damn council let him get away with it every time. Turning a perfectly fine piece of land into a kind of private Disneyland. But not on my watch," he said, wagging a warning finger.

"I talked to the person in charge of the planning commission," said Odelia. "And she said that Tab's applications were ticking all the boxes. Though I think she mainly said that because he brought in plenty of tourism to the area, which is good for the local economy."

"Farmers are good for the local economy, but do you think they care? That Julia Ulenberg was making a mockery of the whole planning commission thing." He frowned darkly, beetling brows moving like mobile clouds across a pair of piercing eyes. "I'll bet she was taking bribes from that jumped-up little songbird. There's no other explanation."

"It's safe to say you weren't a big fan of Tab Fitch or his plans for this land," said Chase. "And you were seen coming from the direction of his house at the time of his murder."

"I didn't kill him, if that's what you're saying."

"You had an excellent motive, Mr. Plontek, and you were right there when it happened."

"I already told you, they didn't allow me anywhere near the house."

"Security wasn't as tight as you suggest," said Chase. "In fact the person in charge of Tab's security was in the bar all morning, drinking himself silly. So looks like the road was clear for an enterprising man like yourself to gain access to the place. Plus, you would have known exactly where to find Tab, from keeping tabs on him and what he was up to."

The farmer glowered at Chase for a moment, then finally said, "This conversation is over, detective. I'd like you to leave now."

"I haven't finished," said Chase.

"Oh, yes, you have. If there's anything else you want to ask me, I suggest you talk to my lawyers. And now get lost, both of you!"

And since he didn't look like the kind of man to trifle with, we decided to skedaddle.

"Pity we didn't get a chance to talk to Bella again," said

Dooley as we walked away. "Maybe she would have been able to shed some more light on Mr. Plontek's actions."

"Oh, so now you think he might have been involved?" I asked.

"At this point in the investigation it's best to keep our options open, Max," said my friend, earning himself a grin from me. "And he certainly looks like a prime suspect to me."

We'd just arrived back on Tab's land when one of the people in charge of security came hurrying over to us. He was a beefy guy we hadn't met before. "We caught two people crawling over the fence," he said. "A woman with blue hair and her husband."

"Where are they?" asked Chase.

"I put them in The Cedars—next to the main house. It's our main guest house."

"How are you fixed for security around the place?" asked Chase. "How many people?"

"Only three right now, me included. Tab only just got back from the Bahamas, and so the skeleton crew he hired to keep an eye on the place is all we've got. He was hiring, though, and planned to bump the team up to seven full-timers."

"I wanted to ask you about Dunton Plontek."

"The crazy neighbor," said the guy with a grimace.

"He put a cow in your charge's pool this morning."

"Yeah, like I said, we're short-staffed at the moment. Apart from Saul, I was the only one here this morning, walking the perimeter to make sure no one got in. But it's a pretty big place, several acres, and one man really isn't enough."

"What about CCTV, electric fencing, security doors?"

"We've got CCTV in place, but not enough manpower to monitor the footage, Tab didn't believe in electric fencing. He wanted a tall Leylandii hedge all around to keep people out, but that takes time, since parts of it were only recently planted. And he was thinking about installing doors with security badges everywhere, those were in the planning stage, awaiting offers from suppliers." He heaved a deep sigh. "We told Tab to beef up security, at least until the rest of the measures had been put in place, but he couldn't be bothered. Said Hampton Cove isn't exactly Chicago or Detroit."

"Can you check your CCTV footage for this morning? Let's say everything one hour before and after twelve. You do record everything?"

"Yes, we do," said the man, looking sheepish. Though if what he said was true, Tab should have been more diligent about putting measures in place to secure his own safety.

CHAPTER 11

"Max, it's candy girl!" Dooley said nervously. "Please, whatever you do, don't take any candy from her!"

"Trust me, I won't, Dooley," I said. Though when we finally caught up with her and her husband, Xanthe and Rasheed didn't look all that eager to dispense with any candy. They were slumped on a large couch, being watched by a large security man who had one of those mics sticking out of his ear and wearing very snazzy sunglasses indoors for some reason. Maybe he had eye issues. He had planted himself in front of the couple, assuming a wide-legged stance, hands behind his back, and looked like one of the men in black.

"Oh, hi," said Xanthe when we walked in, animation returning to her pale face. She'd clearly recognized Odelia. "Can you tell Captain Beefcake over there that we aren't terrorists but honeymooners? He seems to think we're here to set off a dirty bomb."

"It's all right," said Chase to the guy, and flashed his badge. The guy gave a brief nod and left the room.

"So we meet again," said Odelia, not unpleasantly. "You were caught trying to crawl over the fence?"

"It wasn't live," said Xanthe's husband, looking even unhappier now than he had this morning when his wife had suggested to him they hike down to her idol's compound. "What's the point of installing an electric fence when you're not going to run any juice through it? Anyone could have snuck in here and have a pop at Tab."

"Which is exactly what happened," said Chase, dragging up a chair and taking a seat.

Rasheed frowned. "What do you mean?"

"Haven't you heard?" asked Odelia.

"Heard what? My provider decided to cut me off last night," said Xanthe. "I'm on a limited data plan."

"Me, too," said Rasheed.

"So now I can't even Whatsapp my folks or upload my videos to my Insta. Oh, and can you ask them to give us back our phones? Last time I looked this isn't North Korea, and we haven't done anything wrong."

"You mean like scaling a fence and trespassing on private property?" asked Chase.

"It's our honeymoon!" Xanthe said, as if that gave her the right to break into Tab's compound. "I'm Tab's biggest fan, and if only I could talk to him, I'm sure he'd understand."

"When exactly did you arrive?" asked Chase.

The couple shared a look. "Like... half an hour ago?" said Rasheed.

"I met you this morning in Hampton Cove," said Odelia. "When you set out on your hike."

"Yeah, we kinda got lost on the way," said Xanthe with a goofy grimace. She took her husband's hand and gave it a gentle massage. "Like I said, we're on a limited data plan and so we printed out a map at the internet café."

"We must have taken a wrong turn somewhere," said

Rasheed, "and ended up going in a completely different direction." He eyed his wife with a not-so-friendly expression, clearly blaming her.

"It was the old lady!" said Xanthe. "She told us to keep going straight."

"She told us to take a right turn at the next crossroads, then to keep going straight."

"I don't think so."

"And I do."

"I told you we should have changed providers."

"One gigabyte should have been enough."

"YouTube takes up a lot of bandwidth, sweetie."

"I told you not to watch so many YouTube movies!"

"I had to prepare for our meeting with Tab."

"By watching all of his videos? Again?"

"Look, it doesn't matter," said Chase, holding up his hand. "So you say you arrived at the compound at one-thirty?"

"Yeah, something like that," said Xanthe, crossing her arms and throwing a scowl at her husband. "I still don't see why we're being interrogated by the cops. We've done nothing wrong."

"The reason you're being interviewed right now is because Tab Fitch was murdered," said Chase, deciding to come right out and lay the shocking truth on the young couple and see how they'd respond. "And right now you two are both suspects in his murder."

Two jaws dropped, and while tears sprang to Xanthe's eyes, Rasheed looked a lot less impressed by the singer's sudden and shocking demise.

"Tab is dead?" he asked. "You mean, like, someone shot him?"

"I'm afraid I can't go into any details," said Chase. "But yes, Tab is dead."

"But… that can't be!" Xanthe wailed. "He can't be dead!"

"So you actually think that we did it?" asked Rasheed. "But we wouldn't. I mean, why would we want to kill the guy? Xanthe is like his biggest fan on the planet or something."

"Omigod!" said Xanthe, who'd grabbed her face and was rocking back and forth. "Omigod, omigod, omigod, this isn't happening! Who would do such a thing!"

"Probably one of the neighbors," said Rasheed. "Guy was always fighting with his neighbors, buying up property all over the place and building where he wasn't supposed to."

"This is a nightmare!" Xanthe cried. "I've just landed in my worst possible nightmare!"

"It's all right, honey," said her husband, who seemed almost gleeful now at the news that Tab was dead. "It's an occupational hazard with these rock stars that they die young. Drugs, pills, booze—it comes with the territory."

"Not Tab! He was the most level-headed guy on the planet!"

Her husband had placed a comforting arm around her shoulder and she was now wailing into his chest.

"Instead of looking at us," said Rasheed, "you should be looking at Pino Seeds."

"Pino Seeds?" asked Chase. "Who's he?"

Now it was Odelia's turn to stare at her husband. "You don't know Pino Seeds? He's only one of the biggest stars that came out of the glam rock wave in the seventies."

"Never heard of him," said Chase. "The seventies, you say? So he's, like, old?"

"He's not so young anymore," Rasheed conceded. "But still going strong."

"Wasn't he doing a big farewell tour or something?" asked Odelia.

"Yeah, but then he's been doing a farewell tour for the past ten years," said Rasheed. "He's like the Stones, you know. Every time they go on tour people say it's the last one."

"Okay, so why would Pino Seeds want to murder Tab Fitch?" asked Chase. "Enlighten me."

"Pino Seeds is the person who discovered Tab," said Rasheed. "He's the one who gave him his first big break. Was instrumental in landing him a record deal, let him open for him at his concerts and generally acted like a mentor to him. Until Tab became a big star in his own right, and pretty much left Pino in the dust. Now Tab is the one who's raking in the big bucks, and Pino can't even fill a stadium. In fact last I heard Tab, probably feeling sorry for the guy, had offered Pino to open for him on his next tour, coming full circle."

"So you're saying that this Pino Seeds character was feeling resentful?"

"If the snarky comments on his Facebook are anything to go on, absolutely. He called Tab a wannabe copycat and an ungrateful little so-and-so. I'd show you the video but I don't have my phone. And even if I had, I don't have internet right now, as I've explained."

Odelia surfed on her own phone and following Rasheed's instructions had soon found the video in question. A clearly intoxicated elderly man was ranting and raving and calling Tab all kinds of opprobrious names.

"He does look familiar somehow," said Chase, paying close attention.

"Of course he does," said Odelia. "*Carina? Uptown Blues?* He's a major star."

"Not a fan, I'm sorry," said Chase with a shrug. "So where is he now, this Pino Seeds?"

"Staying in town, actually," said Rasheed. "He and Tab had reportedly been working on some new material together. In fact Pino was going to do a duet on Tab's next album."

"So looks like they patched things up, then?" asked Odelia.

Rasheed shrugged. "Who knows? I read that Tab was upset when the video surfaced, and that it took a lot of persuading by his record company to agree to do the duet."

"I don't think Pino would have harmed a hair on Tab's head," said Xanthe, who seemed to have recovered a little from her initial shock. "Pino loves Tab like a son. So he's a little bitter, but that's only to be expected. Pino's career was winding down while Tab's was just getting started. Like *A Star is Born*? Only without the romance, obviously."

Rasheed grinned. "Though I imagine Pino wouldn't have minded a bit of romance."

"Okay," said Chase, tapping the phone. "Thanks for this, but let me warn you that this doesn't mean you two are off the hook. So don't leave town, and stay available for further questioning, all right?"

"Are you not going to arrest us?" asked Xanthe, eyes wide.

"No, I'm not going to arrest you."

"Thank God," said Xanthe, clutching a hand to her chest. "I don't want to spend my honeymoon in jail."

"Oh, by the way, if you're looking for suspects," said Rasheed, when Odelia and Chase made to leave, "you might want to talk to a guy called Steve Rovira. Now there's a man who could have killed Tab. He co-wrote practically all of Tab's hits, but according to some fansites Tab had cut him out of a co-writing credit deal, meaning he wasn't getting a cent."

"We don't know that, Rasheed," said Xanthe. "That's all just a bunch of rumor."

"Not if you look at the credits as displayed on Wikipedia or Tab's official YouTube channel. You won't find Rovira's name anywhere, and everyone knows he and Tab worked on those albums together. Some people even say it's actually

Rovira who wrote those hits, or at least the music, with Tab providing the lyrics, and we all know it's the music that stands out, with some of the lyrics sounding like they were written by a five-year-old."

"How can you say that! Tab's words are so deep—so profound—so, so *poignant*!"

"Of course they are," said Rasheed, with all the patience of the much-put-upon husband of a major Tab Fitch fan. "The man was a genius—may he rest in peace."

CHAPTER 12

The Hampton Cove Star is our town's most fashionable and expensive hotel. It's where all the stars go to stay, which is probably where the hotel gets its name from. So it wasn't hard to see why Pino Seeds would be staying there, even though now a faded star. But first we needed to talk to this producer who fell out with Tab over some co-credit stuff.

We found Steve Rovira in his room on the third floor of the hotel. At first he seemed reluctant to let us in, but when Chase flashed his badge, and so did Odelia, he finally agreed to open the door.

He was dressed in a pink satin dressing gown, a pair of spongy white hotel slippers, and had a three-day growth infesting his pale cheeks. He also had bloodshot eyes and smelled of strong liquor, as did his room, which hadn't been aired out for days.

All in all not the kind of environment I wanted to find myself in for too long. Then again, if you're a detective sometimes you have to stomach these foul conditions.

"So Tab is dead, huh?" said the producer as he opened the minibar and took out one of those small bottles and opened it. "Well, I'd say I'm sorry but actually I'm not."

"We heard you and Tab had a business disagreement?" asked Chase.

"I guess you could call it that," said the man, pouring the contents of the little bottle down the hatch, then wincing. I think it's safe to say it wasn't Evian.

"What would you call it?" asked Chase as he let a keen eye travel around the room. It contained a bed, a table and chair, a closet, television and armchair and not much more.

"Being shafted by the one person in the world you thought you could trust? Being used like a sucker? Being cheated out of your most valued property: your creativity?"

"Tab wasn't going to give you co-credit on some of the stuff you worked on together?"

"Much worse. He stole my songs and claimed them as his own. I wrote all of his hits, and he made it out as if he actually wrote them all by himself. Which is the worst thing you can do as an artist when you think about it. It's a violation of the creator's code."

"But why would he do something like that? Wasn't that going to hurt his reputation?" asked Odelia, who'd carefully removed a piece of underwear from the bed and taken a seat.

"The public really doesn't care about that kind of stuff. As far as they know every singer writes their own material, even though almost none of them do. Same way they think actors write their own lines and the director creates the movie's storyline."

"But people in the business know, surely."

"And they don't care either. Besides, it's impossible for me to prove. In the studio it was just me and Tab most of the time, working away at the piano creating the songs. So who's to say who wrote what? Who came up with the chorus or a catchy melody? It's a close collaboration between two people. Though I'd say I probably came up with seventy percent of the stuff and Tab with the rest. He mostly contributed lyrically and I'm responsible for almost all of the melodies and of course the arrangements."

"So why didn't you insist your name appear on the album when it came out?"

"Oh, but I did. Of course I did. Only Tab said it would be a better sell when it appeared as if he was the sole writer. He envisioned himself as the kind of artist who writes, produces, performs and conceives the whole process, you see. The ultimate creative genius, like the artists he admired and wanted to emulate. And of course the record company agreed, figuring they could market the album like a singular work of art. And if my contribution became known, it would only detract from the myth they were trying to create." He dragged a hand through a shaggy mane of hair. "But of course I'm no fool. We had a gentleman's agreement that even though my name wasn't in the credits, I was still going to be paid as if it was. But then suddenly the royalty checks stopped coming, and I got in touch with Tab, wanting to know what was going on. At first he told me it was probably an honest mistake. A bean counter who put the wrong number in the wrong column, or a problem at the bank, but when nothing changed, and he stopped taking my calls, I understood that the problem wasn't with the record company but with Tab himself."

"He reneged on your gentleman's agreement."

"Never in so many words, mind you. The money simply stopped coming."

"And so you contacted a lawyer."

The producer nodded and gazed out the window. "My lawyer got in touch with his lawyer, and so on and so forth, and the upshot is that I won't be getting any more royalty checks. My contribution to Tab's greatest hits, which have sold millions of records and garnered billions of streams, will never be acknowledged. As if I never even existed."

"Is that why you came to Hampton Cove?"

He turned around and darted a longing eye to the minibar. "You can only have your lawyers talk to their lawyers for so long until you realize that the only person who can fix this is Tab himself. So I've been camped out here for the past couple of days, hoping to talk to him face to face and tell him that he's behaved absolutely horribly and to set the record straight. And this time I wanted everything in writing. No more gentleman's agreement. My credit, up there for all the world to see."

"So did you talk to Tab?" asked Odelia.

The man shook his head. "I've been down there, to 'Fitchville' as they call it, built with the money he owes me, I might add, but they told me he doesn't want to see me. I even posted myself in front of the gate, hoping to catch him coming or going, but the only person leaving is Madison. Tab himself stayed holed up in there, refusing to budge."

"Probably afraid to run into you," said Chase.

"Me or anyone else he wronged," said the man bitterly.

"Like Pino Seeds, you mean?"

The producer looked up at the mention of the name. "Oh, you heard that story, did you? Yeah, Pino isn't exactly Tab's biggest fan right now."

"He's staying at this hotel, isn't he?" asked Odelia.

"Yeah, though he mostly sticks to the bar. I don't have the courage to do that. I like to do my drinking in private," said the man with a wan smile.

"Where were you at twelve o'clock, Mr. Rovira?" asked Chase.

"Right here, where I've been for the best part of the past week."

"Anyone who can confirm that?"

"I'm afraid not. I used to be pretty hot back in my heyday, not just with artists but also with the ladies, but ever since I began my quest to bring the world's hottest young pop star to heel it's been a lonely journey. And probably not the smartest move in my career." When Chase merely stared at him, he sighed. "I can see I'm going to have to spell it out for you, detective. No, I did not kill Tab Fitch. I may have been upset with him. I may have thought he was a terrible person for what he did to me and my career, but I did not go over there to shoot him or stab him or whatever happened to him." He quirked an eyebrow. "How did he die, exactly? I couldn't find any details online."

"I'm afraid I can't divulge anything at this point, sir," said Chase.

"Of course you can't," the man murmured.

"What are you going to do now?" asked Odelia, who seemed to feel sorry for the producer.

"Well, I was actually trying to work a deal through a mutual friend."

"Madison?" asked Odelia.

"No, Val Kip, who's a great guy, and who was going to try and do some persuading. He had to tread carefully, though, since he was producing Tab's new album. But he said he'd had an initial conversation, and told Tab that what he was doing was pretty lousy."

"And what did Tab have to say to that?"

"Just what you'd expect. He denied that my contribution was as big as I made it out to be. Said I was just a troublemaker and advised Val to cut me off if he knew what was good for him. But Val, bless him, wasn't giving up so easily.

Said he was going to keep up the fight." He rubbed his tired features. "He actually called me just now. Said he was going to present my case to Madison. See if she's more amenable than her husband was." He smiled a tired smile. "One can only hope, right?"

CHAPTER 13

We caught up with Pino Seeds in the hotel bar, where the formerly famous rock star was nursing a drink and looking a little worse for wear. He'd been pointed out to us by the hotel barman, and even Odelia looked shocked at the man's appearance. Clearly he didn't look anything like he had in his heyday—the seventies and eighties, when his star had shone bright. He was large around the midsection, not to mention extensively pudgy, pasty-faced, and for some reason had dark eyeliner smeared around his eyes. He was wearing glasses of a peculiar design: large and pink and far too big for his face.

"Mr. Seeds?" asked Odelia. "Pino Seeds?"

"No selfies, please," the man slurred, waving a bejeweled hand.

But instead of taking out their phones, the detecting Kingsleys showed their badges.

He focused on them with some effort, then finally looked up at the pair, then down at Dooley and me. "Am I actually seeing two cats?" he asked finally.

"Yes, those are with me, sir," said Odelia.

"Why?" asked the singer. "I mean, for God's sakes, why in heaven's name would you drag two cats around with you? Is this a new thing? Are they police cats? Sniffer cats?"

"No, sir. Just my personal cats who like to follow me around. They're affectionate that way."

"Oh, right," said the singer, awarding Odelia a curious look. "I usually take my dogs with me everywhere I go. They're border terriers. Though I left them home now. And I have to say I miss them terribly. So what brings you here?" Then his face fell. "Oh, of course. Tab's dead, isn't he?" He raised his glass, containing some clear liquid that didn't look like apple juice. "I was just toasting him. He was a nasty little sod, but he didn't deserve to die like that. How did he die, actually? Shot, stabbed... throat sliced from ear to ear and his heart ripped out of his chest?" he added with a hopeful gleam in his eye.

"I'm not at liberty to discuss the details of an ongoing investigation, sir," said Chase. "I'm sure you can appreciate that."

"Oh, of course," said Pino. "What are you having, detective? I'm buying. And don't give me that 'I can't drink while I'm on duty' crap."

"We have a couple of questions for you, Mr. Seeds," said Chase, ignoring the invitation to accept a free drink at this time. "First off, when was the last time you saw Tab?"

"Oh, must be... two days ago? Yeah, I was staying with him up at the compound he built for himself out there. But for some reason he grew tired of my company and threw me out. No idea why. I'd tell you to ask him, but he's probably not in a fit state to answer." He displayed a jolly grin, trying mightily to focus his eyes on Chase. "So what's your poison, young man? Whisky? Gin? Vodka? I'm a G&T man myself, if you must know."

"So you didn't go up to the house today?" asked Chase stoically.

"No, sir, I did not. Whatever you might think of me, I'm not the kind of person who forces his company on another person. I know when I'm not wanted and if I didn't, Tab's last words to me were pretty clear. 'Never darken my doorstep again,' he said. And so I told him he was a horrible little shit, though I might have used stronger language, and repaired hither, to this fine establishment, where so far no one has kicked me out." He raised his glass. "On the contrary, I'd say. They've welcomed me here with open arms."

"You have no idea why Tab kicked you out?" asked Odelia.

"I can take a wild guess if you like," said the aged singer. "The fact that I told him he was a talentless hack probably didn't go down well, and neither did the fact that when he offered to take me on tour with him as his opening act I said he could go lie in a ditch and die. And once again I should point out I used much stronger language, which I don't like to repeat, since there are women and children present." He gave me a distinctly bleary-eyed look at this point, making me take a wild guess and assume I was one of these children.

It was nice of him, of course, not to use coarse language in front of me and Dooley, or Odelia for that matter. But then he was a funny old bird, and looked pretty harmless. Hard to imagine, though, that once he'd been a famous rock star. He looked more like an eccentric grandpa now.

"Look, Tab was under a lot of pressure, I could tell, what with the recordings for the new album running into delays, and the tour coming up, and some problems with his neighbors, but that didn't give him the right to humiliate me like that. His opening act, for crying out loud. He should have been *my* opening act, not the other way around! I've been in this business more than five decades while he's just starting out! It's not fair." He gave Odelia a questioning look, and tentatively reached out a hand, as if to ascertain whether she was real or just a mirage. "I was a star long before Tab was born, wasn't I, darling?"

"Absolutely, Mr. Seeds," said Odelia with some warmth in her voice, showing us she was a fan.

"Call me Pino," said the singer, then took off his glasses and rubbed his eyes, causing his eyeliner to get smeared all over his puffy cheeks. "It's just not fair," he burbled softly. "No fair." He took a swig from his empty glass, and when he realized no liquid was hitting his esophagus, for a moment stared cross-eyed into his glass then finally held it up high. "Can I get a refill here, please? I'm very thirsty, you know."

"Don't you think you've had quite enough, Pino?" asked Odelia.

He stared at her for a moment, then shook his head stubbornly. "No, I haven't."

"We better take you to your room now," she insisted. "Where is it?"

"No, no selfies!" he exclaimed, swiping at her proffered hand. "I don't do them!"

It took Chase and Odelia a while to convince the singer to let them escort him from the bar, but they finally managed, assisted by the bartender, and Dooley and I patiently waited in the lobby while they took him upstairs to his room.

"Why do people drink so much while it's clearly not good for them, Max?" asked Dooley.

"Probably because it makes them feel better," I said.

"He didn't look very happy, and he's been drinking a lot."

"Alcohol makes people forget they're unhappy," I said.

"But why is he unhappy? He's a big star. Or used to be."

"I think it's the used to be part that makes him unhappy."

"Pour guy. Tab shouldn't have kicked him out. That wasn't nice."

"He probably was making a nuisance of himself. Tab must have been fed up."

"Still. He's just a sad old man. He could have allowed him to hang around. Or maybe even sing a song with him on his new album. A duel, you know."

"A duet, you mean."

"Yeah, that, too."

CHAPTER 14

Chase and Odelia had finally returned to the lobby, when suddenly there was a commotion. The two receptionists behind the desk erupted into nervous chattering, with one hurrying from behind her desk and in the direction of the elevator, which had just disgorged the Pino Seeds rescue party.

"What's going on?" asked Chase, immediately aware of the disturbance. "Police," he added for good measure, and flashed his badge.

The receptionist darted a quick glance back to her colleague, who nodded nervously. "It's the couple in 4B," she said. "The people from the next room are saying they can hear shouts and screams. Sounds like they're in a fight. They're honeymooners," she said, as if that might serve to explain things.

"We'll join you," said Chase immediately, and so we all filed into the elevator.

"Honeymooners?" said Dooley. "Do you think it's candy girl again?"

"I'm sure there's more than one honeymooning couple in

the world," I said, but I had a strange premonition that my friend just might be right. What were the odds?

"What are their names?" asked Odelia.

"Um, Bergson," said the receptionist. "I don't recall their first names…"

"Xanthe and Rasheed?"

"Yes, that's them." Her eyes had widened in surprise. "How did you know?"

"We've had dealings with them earlier today," said Chase with a grim look.

"Oh," said the woman, and it was clear she was expecting the worst now.

Dealings. That could be anything. Especially when the police were involved.

We arrived on the top floor, where apparently the Bergsons were staying. "The honeymoon suite," the receptionist explained helpfully. "Compliments of the house."

"How did that happen?" asked Chase as we all sped along the corridor.

"They won a competition for honeymooners. Free all-inclusive stay."

"Lucky Bergsons," Chase grunted.

As we approached, we could already hear the ruckus. The people from the next room had stepped out into the corridor, and were eagerly awaiting us. They were an elderly couple. "They threw something," said the woman. "Maybe a chair. I heard it hit the wall."

"Oh, dear," said the receptionist, then knocked on the door of the room in question. "Mr. and Mrs. Bergson?" she asked, her mouth close to the panel. "Is everything all right in there?"

The voices, which had been loud and querulous, suddenly fell away.

"Can you please open the door?" the receptionist insisted.

"Go away!" the voice of Xanthe came. "We haven't ordered room service!"

"There's been a complaint. I just want to see if you're okay."

"Just get lost!" the voice of Rasheed now came. "We're fine!"

At this point Chase lost his patience. "This is the police!" he boomed, pounding the door with his fist. "If you don't open this door right now I'm breaking it down!"

"Oh, please don't," the receptionist said, looking aghast at the prospect.

But lucky for her, more sensible sentiments prevailed, and the door was finally opened. Xanthe peered out at us, and when she recognized Odelia and Chase, even seemed relieved. "Oh, hi," she said, a lot less belligerent than before. "What do you want?"

"There has been a noise complaint," the receptionist explained. She tried to look past the blue-haired Tab Fitch fan. "Did you break any furniture?"

"Oh, no," said Xanthe in soft tones. "Well, maybe a chair. But it was already a little broken to begin with. One of the legs was crooked and finally gave way." She now opened the door wider, and we were treated to a room through which clearly a hurricane had passed. Furniture and suitcases had been flung about, with clothes now everywhere, and even one of the curtains seemed to have been torn down. The TV was on the floor, and one of the mattresses was upright against the window, as if it had been picked up by an unseen hand and carelessly dropped where it fell.

"Oh, my God," said the receptionist. "Sir, are you hurt?"

Rasheed was sitting on the remaining mattress, pressing a towel to his face. I thought I could see blood, but it was hard to know for sure.

"I'm all right," he said, sounding a little dispirited.

"He took a seat on the chair and it... collapsed," said Xanthe, doing her utmost to sound upbeat and chipper. "So he hit his head against the cupboard. Just a small cut."

"But the television, the curtains, the mattress," said the receptionist, sounding breathless. "I'm afraid I'll have to report this to the manager, miss."

"Please don't," said Xanthe. "We're newlyweds. We were just having fun." She gave a cheeky wink, but instead of relaying the kind of innocent fun newlyweds might be up to on their honeymoon, it came across as the kind of wink a serial killer might produce when being interrupted in the middle of dismembering his next victim in the bathtub.

For a moment, there was silence, then the receptionist said, with finality, "I'm calling the manager," and stalked off to place the call.

Xanthe sort of crumpled, then went over to sit next to her husband on the bed.

"What happened here, exactly?" asked Odelia.

"She had sex with Tab," said Rasheed with a fiery look at his beloved.

"Just the once," said Xanthe.

"Once is enough."

It was clear from Xanthe's expression, though, that she didn't share this opinion.

"You should get that looked at, son," said Chase, who'd carefully removed the towel and checked the nasty cut the young man had sustained on his cheek. It was bleeding profusely, but then facial cuts often do—or so I've been told. "You'll need stitching."

Before long, the manager arrived on the scene, took one look at the room and sprang into action. Xanthe was escorted from the room and led down to his private office, Rasheed was taken to see a nurse, who could stem the bleeding and stitch up that nasty cut, and the person in charge of housekeeping was summoned to start making an inventory of the room, and to determine the damages the couple would have to pay.

Odelia and Chase, meanwhile, sat with Xanthe, anxious to find out what had caused this sudden violent rift between the erstwhile happy couple.

"I should never have told him," said Xanthe. "But I wanted to be honest, you know. Start our life together without any lies between us."

"So you told him you slept with Tab," said Odelia.

"Just the once!"

"When was this?"

"Three years ago. After one of his shows. I'd won a backstage pass and I got to meet him. For some reason he took a shine to me and as I was leaving along with the others, his personal assistant gave me his phone number. Said to be at his hotel at midnight and he'd let me in through the back entrance. So of course I went." She sighed happily. "It was the most magical night of my life. He was amazing. The most gentle, generous lover you can imagine. Very skilled, too. The things he did with his tongue—"

"Yes, you don't have to give us a detailed account," said Chase hastily.

"Were you already together with Rasheed at the time?" asked Odelia.

"Yeah, I was, but this was Tab Fitch. I wasn't going to miss that chance, was I?"

"And you never told Rasheed about that night?"

"No, of course not. He would have been jealous. Well, you see how he reacted now. Started throwing televisions and chairs around like some crazy person." Her lips turned down into an expression of disapproval. "How can I be with a person like that? A person who doesn't even allow me to enjoy the most magical night of my life?"

"But… Rasheed is your husband," Odelia pointed out.

"He won't be my husband for much longer. Not after this."

"You're going to leave him?"

"Of course! You don't think I'd stay with a person who doesn't understand?"

"Understand what?" asked Chase, having a hard time empathizing.

"Understand what Tab means to me. He's the most important man in my life. Always will be." She sighed a sad little sigh. "I would have had his baby, but he insisted on using protection. I tried to remove it, but he wouldn't let me. Said he was afraid of STDs." She studied her fingernails and so didn't notice how we were all staring at her. Then she frowned. "Rasheed just kept saying I'm the only one of Tab's fans who is so completely crazy about him and it makes him look like a fool, but there's others that think the man was like a god or something." She looked up. "There's actually a family of Tab fans staying at the hotel, and they loved Tab even more than I did, if that's humanly possible."

"Who?" asked Chase, though it was clear his opinion of Xanthe had reached a low.

"Why, the Whiskers, of course."

Dooley looked at me, and I looked at him, our whiskers buzzing with anticipation.

CHAPTER 15

The Whiskers turned out to be an actual family, not the familiar feline appendages. There was Carly Whisker, the mom, Alan Whisker, the dad, Deana Whisker, the sister, and finally, and most importantly, Ray Whisker, who was a little boy of six suffering a terrible disease called spinal muscular atrophy. We met them all in the hotel restaurant, which was pretty much empty at this point in the day, and they were a lovely bunch I have to say.

"Yes, we participated in the *Adopt a Treasure* show last year," said Carly, who had an abundance of curly hair and also an abundance of energy. "Alan wasn't really all that excited when we were accepted but I thought it could be fun, you know."

Alan, a sallow-faced nervous little man who looked like an accountant, bobbed his head. "I didn't see the benefit of parading Ray all over national television, but I have to admit it had some unexpected benefits."

"We were adopted by Tab Fitch, which was just…" Carly smiled a radiant smile. "Possibly the best day of my life. When I heard that gong and Tab came walking out onto the stage. He was so nice, you know. And when the show was over, he said he'd fallen in love with our little boy, and wanted to do whatever he could to make his wish come true."

"And what was your wish, Ray?" asked Odelia.

Ray, who was in a wheelchair and looked as small and pale as could be, smiled a weak smile. "To be Tab's best friend."

"He's always been a big fan of Tab," said Alan.

"Spinal muscular atrophy is a rare genetic disease," said Deana. She was a quiet girl of fifteen, and hadn't yet spoken. "It causes rapid loss of motor neurons, leading to problems with breathing, swallowing and movement."

"There is a drug that treats it called Zolgensma," said Carly. "But it costs two million dollars for a single infusion. Tab said he was going to pay for everything. He promised to put Ray up at the best hospital where he would receive the best treatment. We couldn't possibly pay for it, though our own doctor is great and has been fighting for Ray hard all this time."

"Dr. Ryburn is the best," said Alan in flat tones.

"He is the best, but there's best and then there's better," said his wife. "And with Tab's help chances of our little boy beating this thing have become a lot better, haven't they?"

"He said he's going to write a song for me," said Ray. "And put it on his new album. The song will be called *Ray's Song*, and he already sang a little bit of it for us on Skype."

"And it sounded... absolutely wonderful!" Carly gushed. "I had tears in my eyes, I kid you not. Tears of absolute joy. Tab is going to release *Ray's Song* as a single and all the proceeds are going to his treatment, which is due to start next month."

"So you're here in town to talk about this with Tab?" asked Odelia.

"Absolutely. Tab invited us and we're patiently waiting for him to get in touch. Isn't that right, Whiskers?"

"Absolutely," said Ray.

"So why aren't you staying at Tab's compound?" asked Chase.

"Just a minor misunderstanding," said Carly. "We're in the process of getting that all worked out."

"You have heard about what happened to Tab, haven't you?" asked Odelia.

Carly and Alan both turned to Ray and Carly said hurriedly, "Deana, will you take your brother for his walk now?"

"But I don't want to go for a walk," said Ray. "I want to hear about Tab."

"We'll tell you all about it in a minute, darling," said Carly, as she touched her son's cheek.

"Oh, all right," said the little boy a little reluctantly. He was wearing a T-shirt with Tab's face printed on it, and wearing a cap that said, 'Tab's #1 Fan.'

His sister wheeled him off, and Carly turned to us. "We haven't told him yet."

"Frankly the news will be devastating, I'm afraid," said Alan.

"Sooner or later you'll have to tell him," said Odelia.

"I know, but we're still trying to figure out how," said Carly.

"Also, we don't know what's going to happen now that Tab is gone," said her husband. "With the treatment, I mean. Tab said he was going to pay for everything, but now that he's dead, are his next of kin going to honor his agreement? It's all up in the air now."

"I'm sure Madison will do the right thing," said Odelia. "We met her this morning and she seems like a really nice person."

"We haven't met Madison yet," said Carly, "but your words are exactly what we needed to hear right now, Mrs.

Kingsley. I won't conceal from you that we've been more than a little worried ever since we read the first reports about Tab's death. It's a major blow."

"Dr. Ryburn is a great doctor," said Alan, "but he can only do so much."

"Tab really was our last hope," said Carly.

"The results of this drug are very impressive," said Alan. "We need this to happen. If not..." His voice broke, and he took his wife's hand in his and pressed it.

It was clear to me now that Carly's relentless optimism was underpinned with a powerful sense of desperation that was clearly shared by her husband and my heart bled for the Whiskers.

And we would have talked more, but just then there was a high-pitched scream somewhere nearby, and the few people present in the restaurant all rushed over to the window to see what was going on.

We just reached there in time to see that a man had apparently fallen from one of the upstairs windows, and had landed on the hotel entrance canopy, bounced once and dropped on top of a waiting cab, where he now lay motionless, sprawled on his back.

When I looked a little closer, I saw that it was none other than... Pino Seeds!

CHAPTER 16

An ambulance was called and soon arrived, and as Pino was carefully lifted from the cab, he flashed us all a radiant smile—or at least as radiant a smile as any man who's just fallen from three stories high can be expected to make. He even waved to what he probably perceived as his adoring fans.

"I'll be back, my lovelies," he said a little weakly. "I'll be announcing my comeback tour very soon now. Tickets to be sold everywhere. Don't miss it. It's going to be a big splash!"

And then he was carted off in the ambulance to the nearest hospital.

We all glanced up to the window of the aged rock singer's room. Had he fallen, had he jumped or was he pushed? Hard to determine at this stage. Though judging from the state the man was in, he simply could have stepped out onto the balcony and lost his balance. Just to be sure, Chase and Odelia joined the hotel manager to check out the man's room.

It was a nice room, as rooms go, and certainly a damn sight better than the one where Steve Rovira was currently holed up. It wasn't the honeymoon suite, but it still consisted of more than just the one room. When we arrived there, we saw that the window to the balcony was open, the curtains billowing gently in the breeze.

Chase and Odelia stepped out and carefully surveyed the scene.

"No signs of a struggle," Chase determined finally. "Don't think he was pushed."

Odelia had crouched down and retrieved a bottle of gin that was lying underneath a chair. She'd donned a plastic glove for the occasion and held up the bottle for our inspection. It was empty.

"If he drank the whole bottle, on top of what he'd already had to drink downstairs, it stands to reason he toppled over the railing," said Chase.

The hotel manager, who'd briefly inspected the room for damage, seemed satisfied that at least Pino Seeds wasn't in the same category as the Bergsons, who'd managed to partially destroy his precious honeymoon suite. When he caught sight of the empty bottle, he frowned. "That's exactly why I don't like to rent rooms to rock stars," he said with a disapproving eye. "If they're not inviting groupies to organize orgies, they use their guitars to smash up the furniture. Can you believe we once had a rock star who found nothing better to do than to smear his own fecal matter on all the walls and furnishings? Took us ages to get out the foul stench. Suffice it to say we put him on our blacklist."

"What's fecal matter, Max?" asked Dooley.

"Doo-doo, Dooley," I said.

My friend's eyes widened. "Why would anyone want to use his own doo-doo as paint? Is it a new trend in home decorating, you think? Some European thing?"

"I very much doubt that. Though it could be some new art form."

"Have you had trouble with Pino Seeds before?" asked Odelia.

"He's never fallen out of a window before, if that's what you mean."

"No, I suppose we would have heard if he had. Well, thank you," she said.

"Will you keep me informed? I'd like to know if he's coming back or not."

"He did say he was making a comeback, didn't he, Max?" said Dooley.

"He most certainly did," I said. Though somehow I doubted if he would.

Just then, Chase's phone belted out a chime and he picked up with a grunted, "Kingsley." Then he frowned. "We'll be there in ten." He flicked off his phone and directed a startled look at his wife. "That was Dolores. Dunton Plontek has gone off his rocker. He's threatening to level Fitchville with a bulldozer."

🐾

It actually took us less than ten minutes to head out to Fitchville, and when we arrived there we saw that Chase hadn't lied: Mr. Plontek was indeed in a bulldozer, and was indeed hurling abuse at the inhabitants of Tab's newly found community even as the bulldozer's powerful engine belched out fumes and the farmer seemed ready, willing and able to drive the large contraption into the compound and do some serious damage.

"He arrived here about half an hour ago," Madison Fitch explained when we joined her. "Said if the council won't start demolishing this illegally built community he's going to take the law into his own hands and do it himself." She darted an anxious look at the irate farmer. "Do you think he's bluffing or is he actually going to level the place?"

"He does look as if he means business," said Odelia.

Meanwhile, Chase had walked up to the bulldozer and waved at Mr. Plontek to stop this nonsense forthwith. Of course the farmer refused even to acknowledge the cop.

Next to Madison, Darnell stood, unhappy at these proceedings, and also Saul Goff, who looked bleary-eyed, as if he was nursing a terrible headache. There was also a third man I'd never seen before. This was presumably Tab's producer Val Kip, the man Steve Rovira had been in contact with to convince Tab to let Mr. Rovira have his royalties back. He was a tall man with fashionable glasses, a fashionable little beard and fashionably dressed.

"Is that..." Odelia began.

"Val Kip," Madison confirmed. "Tab's producer."

Odelia sidled up to the producer and held out her hand. "Odelia Kingsley," she said. "I'm a police consultant, assisting with their inquiries into the death of Tab Fitch."

"Val Kip," said the man with a curt nod of the head. He gestured to the man in the bulldozer. "How long is this going to take?"

"Oh, I'm sure my husband will be able to talk Mr. Plontek off the ledge," said Odelia. "He can be very convincing."

"That's your husband over there?"

"Chase Kingsley. He's the detective in charge of the investigation."

The producer nodded and adjusted his glasses. "Terrible business," he murmured sympathetically. "I haven't known Tab long, of course, but by all accounts the man was a genius."

"Was the record you were making almost done?"

"Well, the songs had all been written, but we'd only just started our recording sessions."

"So there will be no album?"

"No, unfortunately not. There are demos, of course, but the quality is not what you would call up to standard. Though I can imagine the record company will still try and salvage what they can. Maybe release a couple of the songs."

"I've heard they sometimes bring in another singer when the original singer dies?"

"Oh, absolutely. But it's never going to be the same. Tab had a unique voice. He was a singer-songwriter in the truest sense of the word. Liked to do everything himself. Played a lot of the instruments, even did some of the backing vocals. Nowadays a lot of these so-called pop stars can't even sing, let alone play an instrument or write a song. They buy their songs in bulk from a couple of professional hit factories, often in Sweden, then hire a top producer who can work around the deficiencies in their voices."

"But not Tab."

"Oh, no. Tab was the real deal."

"We talked to Steve Rovira this morning," said Odelia. "He's been trying to get Tab to acknowledge the role he played in the creation of his first two albums. He also said you were acting as a kind of middleman between himself and Tab?"

Val glanced over to Odelia, sizing her up. "Does this have any bearing on Tab's death?"

"It might have. We're trying to form as complete a picture of Tab as we can. And if he cheated his former producer out of a co-writing credit, it might be a motive for murder."

"Yes, I imagine so," said the man vaguely. He sighed. "Well, it's true, of course. There was a lot of bad blood between Steve and Tab and I was trying to nudge Tab in the direction of a solution that would benefit them both. I tried to explain to Tab that denying Steve's role in the creation of his first two albums was going to hurt him in the long run. The music business is a small world, Mrs. Kingsley, and people talk. Already there are people out there who refused to work with Tab. Musicians, other singers, producers. Exactly because of the way he treated Steve. So yes, I was trying to work out a solution."

"What's going to happen now that Tab is dead?"

The producer gestured to Madison. "Now it's up to Tab's widow, I guess. I suppose she'll inherit not only Tab's material possessions but also his immaterial ones."

"Like his royalties."

Val nodded. "And knowing Madison I think she'll be amenable to a compromise."

Who wasn't amenable to a compromise was Dunton Plontek, for the bulldozer's engine was now roaring like a wounded animal, and he suddenly advanced a couple of inches in our direction, causing the small gathering to let out horrified cries.

"He's going to run us all down, Max!" said Dooley. "We have to talk to Bella!"

"What is Bella going to do?" I asked.

"He's a farmer, isn't he? And farmers love their cows. So if we drag Bella out here, and make her take a stand, he'll just have to stop. He's not going to run her down, is he?"

There was a sort of logic in what he said. Then again, how do you get a cow to go and stand in front of a bulldozer? Cows may not be the smartest creatures, but they're not crazy. No way was she going to be convinced to play the role Dooley was envisioning for her.

"Get down here at once!" Chase was now bellowing at the recalcitrant farmer. In response, Dunton pressed his foot down on the gas and made his bulldozer rumble and roar. And when Chase tried to mount the bulldozer and bodily drag the man from his perch in the bulldozer cabin, he discovered that Dunton had latched the door shut.

"So can I ask you one more question, Mr. Kip?" said Odelia.

"Sure," said the producer.

"Can you tell me where you were at twelve o'clock?"

"If you must know, I was sleeping in. Tab had me up all night, and frankly I was completely bushed. I only woke up when one of the housekeepers came into my room and told me something had happened in the studio. By the time I arrived there Tab was already dead and the place was crawling with police. Wouldn't let me anywhere near."

"Can anyone vouch for you, sir?" asked Odelia dutifully.

"If you're asking me if I slept alone, then yes, I did."

"You're not married?"

"I was, but the music business is not conducive to marital bliss, I'm afraid. My wife finally couldn't take the long days I habitually spend in the studio and the fact that sometimes she didn't see me for weeks or even months at a time."

Odelia gave him a look of commiseration. "How long were you planning on working on Tab's new album?"

The producer shrugged. "Could have been weeks, months... Tab signed a contract to deliver the new album's masters last month, actually, but he got delayed."

"He spent a couple of weeks in the Bahamas writing the new songs, I believe?"

"He was supposed to finish them last fall, with recording scheduled for the winter and the album ready in the spring. But that didn't happen. And now it never will."

Madison Fitch clearly had had enough of this charade, and now approached the bulldozer. Chase helped her up, and we all watched, wondering what this petite lady hoped to accomplish. But lo and behold: as she yelled something to the farmer that we couldn't hear, the man opened the door of his dangerous contraption an inch, and moments later, we saw that he was nodding in agreement, and switched off the engine.

He then climbed down from the large machine, along with Madison, and as we looked on, the two shook hands, with the farmer even displaying something that might be construed as a smile. He then climbed back into his dozer and moments later was backing away, before slowly trundling down the road, back to where he came from.

We all grouped around Madison. "What did you say to him?" asked Darnell.

Tab's widow shrugged. "I made him an offer on his farm and he accepted."

"You're going to buy Plontek's farm?" asked Saul. "But why?"

"Because that's what Tab would have wanted," said Madison simply.

"But I thought he didn't want to sell?" said Odelia. "That's why he was so upset?"

"Oh, he definitely wanted to sell," said Madison. "He just wasn't happy with the price Tab was offering."

"How much did you offer?" asked Darnell.

"Twice the market price," said Madison.

"Twice!" Saul cried. "But that's crazy!"

"So that's why he was smiling," said Chase.

"I've never seen a farmer smile before, Max," said Dooley. "I didn't think they had it in them."

"Tab only wanted to go as high as twenty percent over the market price," said Madison, "which is why this thing kept dragging on for so long." Her face clouded. "Maybe if he'd gone along with what Plontek was asking, my husband would still be alive."

"You really think Plontek is responsible for Tab's murder?" asked Odelia.

"I don't know," said Madison, giving her a keen look. "Is he?"

An apt question, of course. Had the farmer killed Tab to get what he wanted? And had Madison played into the man's hands by offering him twice the going rate for his property?

Tough questions, and the only ones who could get the answers were Chase and Odelia.

"So you're going to keep Fitchville?" asked Darnell as we walked back to the house.

"I think so," said Madison. "Fitchville was Tab's dream. I might complete the project and open it up to the public at some point. Turn it into a convention center or a museum." She shrugged. "I don't know. Too soon to tell, Darnell."

"Of course," said Tab's cousin, and placed an arm around the widow's shoulder.

Hard to imagine that Tab had only died that morning. Somehow it seemed longer.

CHAPTER 17

I have to say I was more than happy to be home again that night. It had been a long day, with plenty of interviews and a lot that had happened in a short space of time. When we arrived home I was surprised to find Harriet and Brutus gone, even though Harriet had said she wasn't going to leave the house all day, due to her horoscope.

"See?" said Dooley. "You didn't take the candy and you're fine, Max. So tomorrow you have to ask Harriet what the horoscope says before we leave the house. It's very important."

"Do you think Harriet's astrologer can also tell us who killed Tab Fitch?" I asked.

"Do you really think so?" said Dooley, his excitement immediately roused.

"No, I don't," I said. "I was just kidding, Dooley."

"You know what I find odd? That Tab and Madison don't have pets. These pop stars usually have at least one pet, don't they? I mean, when you check their Instagram it's always full of them."

He was right, of course. When you check Taylor Swift's

Instagram you can't look past her cats. And Katy Perry's dogs are usually well represented on her social media. But of Tab's pets there was not a single trace. Okay, so the man was allergic to cats, but surely not to all pets.

"Maybe Tab didn't like pets," I said.

"You think so? A man like him, with that weird compound he was building for himself and his family, should have at least a private petting zoo or something."

"Tab Fitch isn't Michael Jackson, Dooley. He doesn't have pet snakes or a pet chimp."

"Yeah, I guess that kind of thing isn't done anymore. Though Fitchville does remind me of Neverland, Max."

"Yeah, it does a little bit, doesn't it?" I said thoughtfully.

Just then, Harriet and Brutus came in through the pet flap. Harriet looked worried. "Oh, hey, you guys," she said. "How did it go today?"

"One murdered pop star, one old rock star who fell from a window and smashed up a cab, one groupie couple who destroyed their hotel room and one producer who's suing to get the rights to his songs back. Otherwise it was a pretty uneventful day."

"Oh, that's great," said Harriet absentmindedly, as if she hadn't even heard what I said. She disappeared into the kitchen, presumably for a litter box break, still looking thoughtful.

"What's wrong with Harriet?" I said.

"Don't ask," said Brutus, but then proceeded, "She got a sneak peek at tomorrow's horoscope through Madame Burnett's fansite. And it doesn't look good, I have to say."

"Why?" asked Dooley, immediately on edge. "What does it say? More candy people?"

"So you remember how today's horoscope said she shouldn't leave the house all day, right?"

We both nodded.

"Well, tomorrow's horoscope says she's going to meet a dark, handsome stranger who's going to set her soul on fire." He arched a meaningful whisker. "And my horoscope says I'm going to meet a pretty brunette who's going to turn my life upside down. So you can see how this looks, can't you?"

"As if… you are both going to fall in love with other people?" I said carefully. I know how jealous both Harriet and Brutus can get, so this didn't bode well for the future.

"Well, I'm the dark, handsome stranger, of course," said Brutus. "And Harriet will meet me the moment she opens her eyes. But the pretty brunette? Now there's a quandary."

"Right," I said, though I didn't see the full picture yet. "Because…." I prompted.

"Because Harriet isn't a brunette, you guys! So who is this brunette who's going to turn my life upside down, huh? And where am I going to meet her and why? I mean, I'm perfectly happy with my life right now, so the notion of having it turned upside down doesn't really hold all that much appeal to me." He sighed and slumped down on his haunches. "I have to say this horoscope business is a tough nut to crack."

"So how about my horoscope?" asked Dooley. "And Max's horoscope?"

"I'm sorry, but we didn't really bother," said Brutus. "After the shock we got from reading our own horoscope, you can imagine we didn't look any further."

"No, of course not," I murmured. "Very understandable."

Just then, Harriet returned from her bathroom break. "So did you tell Max?" she asked.

"Yeah, I did."

"What do you think, Max? Who's this mysterious brunette Brutus is going to meet?"

"I have absolutely no idea," I confessed.

"Oh, Max!" she cried, stomping her paw. "And you call yourself a detective!"

"A detective who looks for clues in the real world, Harriet," I said. "Not in la-la land."

"Ever the skeptic, aren't we?" she said with a pout. "I should have known we couldn't count on you."

"Did you read anything about candy?" asked Dooley.

"Oh, Dooley," she said with a quick toss of her head.

I guess Dooley and I would have to wait until the morrow to know our own fate. Not that I was overly worried. Frankly I don't put too much stock in horoscopes or any of that superstitious stuff. And that mysterious brunette that was going to turn Brutus's life upside down was probably a new type of kibble that would make him sick in the tummy.

And as Chase and Odelia started dinner prep, we all settled down on the couch. Harriet and Brutus hovering over the tablet to study some more of their horoscopes, and Dooley and me to catch up on all the naps we'd skipped during the day. And we'd been sleeping peacefully for what felt like hours when I woke up from the sound of a Tab Fitch song playing nearby.

I opened one eye to see that Odelia and Chase were on the couch, watching a piece of documentary about the well-known singer on Odelia's laptop. It appeared to be a home movie of the singer in his studio, thrumming on his guitar and jotting down the odd note.

We all watched on as the now deceased singer was in the midst of composing a new song, his wife Madison looking on with distinct pride written all over her features.

"Imagine being able to write a song from scratch like that," said Odelia. "It probably takes a huge talent to be able to do that."

"It's just a knack," said Chase. "Like riding a bike."

Odelia frowned. "I'm sure writing a hit song is more difficult than riding a bike."

"It's a trick you can learn. There's plenty of sites where they show you how it's done."

"So you're telling me that everyone can write a hit song?"

"Absolutely. You could do it. I could do it."

"Huh. So why doesn't everybody do it?"

"Because they don't know that it's just a trick, babe. Like you, they think it's about talent, when it's not. Like that producer fella told you, there are hit factories where they churn out hundreds of songs. There's people who write a new hit every hour, on the hour."

"Imagine that," said Odelia. "Being able to write hit after hit after hit."

"And then of course there's computer algorithms now who do it for you."

"A computer can write a hit?"

"Why not? It's all about artificial intelligence. Computers can do anything these days. They can drive cars, perform complicated operations, 3D-print livers, and write hits."

"Can a computer also solve a murder?" she asked as she snuggled up to Chase.

"Sure thing. Pretty soon you and me will be obsolete. Some low-level bureaucrat will feed all the information into a computer and out pops the name of the killer. Easy-peasy."

"Imagine that, Max," Dooley marveled. "A computer will solve every crime!"

"Yeah, imagine that," I said, and had a hard time keeping the lack of conviction from my voice. Somehow I had a feeling it wasn't that easy. If it was, we'd live in a crime-free society, and the last time I looked that wasn't the case. Yet.

"Hey, will you look at this," said Odelia.

We all looked up.

"What's this?" asked Chase.

"A Tab Fitch fansite. It says that the new Netflix documentary is canceled."

"Stands to reason," said Chase. "The man is dead."

"No, but this was before he died." She frowned at the screen. "This person claims that it was actually Tab himself who canceled the contract. Said he had a change of heart."

"I wonder why Darnell didn't tell us."

"Maybe he didn't know?"

"He's the one making the documentary. If there's anyone who should know if it was canceled or not it's Darnell."

"Let's ask him about it tomorrow. It's just a fansite. They're probably wrong."

Or they were right and Tab's cousin had lied to us.

CHAPTER 18

That night, cat choir was a festive affair. Turns out that Harriet's obsession with Madame Burnett's site was infectious and everyone had been avidly following that lady's predictions.

"I'm going to be a big star," said Shanille, cat choir's conductor. "Madame Burnett said so this morning. 'Your path is a glittering one, dear one. Strewn with gold and diamonds.' That can only mean we're going to take cat choir international! Fame and fortune awaits us. We're going to sell out Madison Square Garden, then tour the globe. Wembley Stadium in London, the Zenith in Paris, the Colosseum in Rome…"

"I don't think they still use the Colosseum," I offered as a discordant note. "They used to, but that was in Roman times, back when they still had gladiators fighting to the death, and wild animals being killed to satisfy the public's bloodlust."

"Oh, you always have to be a spoilsport, haven't you, Max?" said Shanille, and made a gesture of disgust then trotted off to regale some more gullible soul with her tales of fame and fortune.

"What about you, Dooley?" asked Kingman, one of our best friends. "What does your horoscope say?"

"Just that I have to be quiet," said Dooley, and looked pained. "I haven't exactly been quiet today, though, have I, Max? Do you think I'll be punished now?"

"I doubt it, Dooley," I said. "Madame Burnett probably has better things to do than to go around punishing people that don't do what her horoscope says."

"How about you, Max?" asked Kingman.

"Max has to watch out for people doling out candy," said Dooley. "And he did, and he made it through the day in one piece." He gave me a proud look.

"I don't even like candy," I said.

"My horoscope said I'd meet a dark, handsome stranger and she'd rock my world," said Kingman. "Which is odd, since the only stranger I met today was Wilbur's IRS agent, and he wasn't tall or dark. He stepped on my tail when he walked into the store, so he did rock my world, but not in the way I expected, to be absolutely honest. He also gave Wilbur a big fine, so he rocked his world, too, and he didn't look happy about it."

"So many dark, handsome strangers around," I murmured, casting an amused look in Harriet's direction. Maybe she would meet that same IRS agent tomorrow?

But Harriet paid me no attention. She was too busy sharing her own troubles with her friends, namely about the brunette who was going to turn Brutus's world upside down.

"So how is it going with the investigation?" asked Kingman. "Any progress?"

"Not much," I said. "But it's still early days."

"Max thinks the neighbor did it," Dooley revealed.

"And what do you think, Dooley?" asked Kingman.

"I think the candy people did it, of course. They are vicious!"

"Vicious candy people," said Kingman with a chuckle. "Gotta watch out for those."

"Oh, we will," Dooley assured the big cat. "And I'm watching Max's back, too."

"Good for you, little buddy," said Kingman, patting our friend on his own back.

Just then, Buster came sneaking up to us. He's the hairdresser's Maine Coon. He glanced left and right, then joined us, looking extremely furtive I have to say.

"What's wrong, Buster?" I asked.

"Yeah, you look like you've just seen a ghost," said Kingman.

"It's my horoscope, you guys," he said quietly, his eyes darting about the place like ping pong balls. "It said this morning I have to keep a close eye on the sky. And so I've been doing just that. Only now my neck hurts, and I still don't know why I need to keep an eye on that sky."

"Probably to make sure it doesn't fall down on top of your head," said Dooley, also subjecting that inky sky to a closer scrutiny. "It has been known to happen, you know."

"When the sky falls on our heads we'll all be dead," said Kingman. "So frankly if I were you I wouldn't worry about it, Buster."

Buster gulped, and so did Dooley. "Dead?" asked Buster. "You think so?"

"The sky isn't going to fall, Buster," I assured the cat. "It's safely strapped in place."

"If you say so," he said, but he didn't sound fully convinced.

"I knew I should have kept quiet," said Dooley. "Now I've gone and done it. The sky is going to fall and it'll all be my fault!"

And since frankly I'd heard all about falling skies and other horoscope disasters, I decided to head on home again.

After all, how much lunacy can one take? Not that much. And I was walking home, alone this time, when I thought I heard a soft sound behind me. But when I stopped, it also stopped. And when I started walking again, it also resumed.

I quickly glanced over my shoulder, but didn't see anything or anyone following me.

So I shrugged it off and chalked it up to the general sensation of malaise that had descended on cat choir. Usually cat choir is the one place I can go to relax, and enjoy the pleasant company of my friends, but tonight it had been more a source of annoyance than enjoyment, and I blamed it all on this Madame Burnett, whoever she might be.

And I'd almost reached home when I suddenly heard it again: a silent footfall behind me. So this time I quickly sidestepped the sidewalk and hid underneath a nearby hardy shrub, hoping to catch whoever had been following me. I waited a few moments, and suddenly, and much to my surprise, I saw that it was none other than Harriet!

I emerged from my hiding place and joined her. "Have you been following me?"

She looked startled. "Following you? Of course not. Why would I be following you?"

"But… you were right behind me this whole time."

"And you were right in front of me this whole time, so I think a case could be made that you were following me."

This kind of skewed logic is typical for my Persian friend, and so I decided not to pursue the matter further.

"Something on your mind?" I asked, for she did look out of sorts.

"It's this brunette that Brutus is going to meet, Max. It's driving me nuts, if I'm honest. So far Madame Burnett hasn't been wrong once, and so this time tomorrow my life won't be the same again."

"I think it's just a load of—"

"Please, Max. I know you're a skeptic, but keep your opinions to yourself."

"Fine," I said with a shrug. "But I think you're getting worked up over nothing."

"We'll see." She gave me a sideways glance. "Oh, I probably should have mentioned this, but your horoscope says that you're going to encounter a big surprise tomorrow. It's going to make you sit up and think, but at the end of the day it's going to make you feel grateful for the choices that you've made so far."

"What does that even mean!" I cried.

"I don't know, but you have to admit it sounds intriguing."

"What does Dooley's horoscope say?"

"Nothing special. Just that he needs to learn to appreciate the sound of silence."

"Isn't that what today's horoscope said?"

"So? Silence is not something you can learn in a day, Max. Ask any Buddhist monk."

We were both silent for a moment as we walked on, our paws leading us home of their own accord, after having walked this same route hundreds, maybe thousands of times.

"If Brutus does meet this brunette," said Harriet suddenly.

"Oh, God, not again with the—"

But she shut me up with a single glance. "Can you promise me you'll talk some sense into him? Now I know this brunette will be wonderful, amazing, and will make his heart go pitter-patter."

"Isn't it baby's feet that go pitter-patter?" I asked.

"Whatever. I want you to remind him that he has a loving cat waiting for him at home. Will you do that for me, Max?"

"Of course. But I don't think—"

"Just… do it, all right?"

"Fine," I said with a sigh. "If a dark, handsome brunette

stranger makes his heart go pitter-patter I'll remind him that he has a very nice girlfriend waiting for him at home."

"Not nice, Max," she chided me. "A paw rub is nice. A favorite blanket is nice. Tell him he's got a spectacular girlfriend at home. The love of his life, in fact."

"Okay, all right!" I said, not liking this particular assignment one bit.

"Thanks, Max." She gazed at me for just a second too long. "You're a dear, dear friend."

"You're welcome," I said, starting to dislike this Madame Burnett more every second.

CHAPTER 19

The next morning, bright and early, saw the team back at Fitchville for more of this investigative stuff. This time Chase and Odelia decided to dig a little deeper into the reason why the movie of Tab's life had been canceled—if that fansite was to be believed.

We found Darnell, the intrepid documentary maker, in the gym, where he was working himself into a sweat on the stairmaster. He looked a little bedraggled and very sweaty when we came upon him. He also had dark rings under his eyes, and had clearly had a restless night.

After he slapped a towel around his neck and dried off his perspiration, he took a protein drink from the fridge and took a seat at a nearby table, along with Odelia and Chase.

"Yeah, the film was canceled," he said when prompted. "Tab decided to bail."

"Why didn't you tell us this yesterday?" asked Chase.

The man shrugged and wiped off some more sweat springing from his brow. "I just figured it didn't matter anymore now that he was dead. And also, maybe Madison will feel different. I've talked to her, and she seems prepared to give the project another chance."

"Why did Tab cancel?" asked Odelia.

"He saw some early footage and felt that the movie showed too much private stuff. Stuff he didn't feel comfortable sharing with the rest of the world. Especially some of the home movies I made years back made him cringe."

"But what about the rest? The making of the album? The concert tour?"

Darnell shook his head. "He said no to the whole thing. Said he didn't think people are particularly interested to see how the sausage is made. All they want is the final result. He also thought it was too soon for him to release a concert movie. Said he wasn't ready yet. Maybe in a couple of years, when he was a better artist, he'd give it another shot."

"How did you feel about his decision?"

The man took a long swig from his protein drink, then looked up from beneath lowered eyelids. "How do you think I felt? I was gutted. I worked on this project for years. It was going to be my calling card. The film that would put me on the map. Launch my career. I was furious. Tried to argue with him, but the more I argued, the more he dug his heels in. He could be stubborn that way. So finally I said I'd release the film without his permission. Turn it into an unofficial documentary. Like a fan project, you know. Plenty of people wanted to see it. In fact when we released snippets the response was overwhelmingly positive."

"So what did he say?"

"That if I did that he'd never speak to me again. Also, he'd sic his lawyers on me."

"You must have been very upset."

"Upset doesn't even begin to describe it. When he told me it was as if my whole world came crashing down around me. My entire life spent on this single project: to capture the essence of what made my cousin who he was. His rise to fame. It wasn't fair that he would do that to me. After all the promises he made. After all the work I put into this thing."

"You could have made another movie. About another topic?"

"There is no other topic! I'm Tab Fitch's cousin, for crying out loud. That's what I am. My one claim to fame. Without Tab I'm just a dude with a camera." He slammed the empty can down on the table and rose. "Anything else you want to ask me? I need a shower."

"Is this why you left the compound yesterday looking angry?" asked Chase.

He nodded. "I'd taken another stab at him. Tried to argue my case. But he wasn't having it. Said his mind was made up and if I didn't like it I could always leave. He also didn't allow me to film him anymore. Said there was no point. And besides, it had started to annoy him. Said it impeded his creative process."

"So that's when you snapped and you killed him," said Odelia quietly.

The man's eyes went wide. "What? No! Of course not. Was I angry with my cousin? Absolutely! But I didn't kill him. I loved the guy, even though he could be a real pain in the ass sometimes. No, I left because if I stayed I would have said some pretty nasty stuff, and I didn't want that. So I took myself out of the equation and went for a walk to cool off."

"You can see how this looks, though, can't you, Darnell?" said Chase. "You admit you were extremely upset with your cousin, because he'd singlehandedly wrecked your life's work, even destroyed your life in a sense. Plus you were right there when it happened, so not only did you have a very strong motive to kill your cousin, you also had means and opportunity. In my book that makes you a very solid suspect for his murder."

"But I didn't do it!"

"So who did?"

He grabbed his hair and looked around, clearly distraught. "I… Saul is the person who comes to mind."

"Saul Goff? Why would he kill Tab? He was his best friend."

"Used to be," said Darnell. "Before he found out that Tab was sleeping with Adima."

"Adima?"

"Saul's wife."

"Tab was having an affair with his best friend's wife?"

Darnell nodded. "Saul only found out yesterday, but apparently it's been going on for a while. Safe to say that Saul wasn't too pleased."

"How did he find out?"

"Adima told him over the phone. I was there when she called. Saul was devastated."

CHAPTER 20

Saul Goff looked like a man who was nursing the hangover from hell. Even though it had been almost twenty-four hours since we'd seen him in The Tab, it was safe to say he probably hadn't stopped drinking all day yesterday, and maybe even part of the night. His eyes were watery, his skin mottled and dusted with dark stubble, and I could tell he had a mean headache he was fighting off with some heavy-duty medication that made him sluggish in his responses and slurring his speech.

We met him in the meeting area in front of the orangery where he was enjoying some sunshine and fresh air.

"Yes, my wife was having an affair with Tab. Happy now?"

"Not exactly," said Chase.

The man rubbed his face with a coal shovel of a hand. Hard to imagine anyone having the gall to turn this man into his enemy by sleeping with his wife, but Tab had. With lethal consequences?

"How did you find out?"

"She told me. Yesterday morning. She's in rehab right now. Twelve-step program. The counselor told her to fess up to any transgressions she made in her life, and this was one of them. So she called and just blurted it out then asked for my forgiveness. Which," he said tersely, "she will get the day hell freezes over."

"So when we found you in the bar yesterday…"

He grinned a pained grin. "Ironic, isn't it? My wife is in rehab for alcohol addiction, and as part of her process she tells me the worst possible thing any man wants to hear, and makes me hit the bottle like I've never hit it before in my life. I'm thinking conspiracy here, people. This rehab place she's staying at clearly isn't satisfied with one customer, they want to get me, too. Hey, maybe I'll qualify for a group discount. Family pack."

He sounded flippant, but it was obvious that the man was hurting.

"You had no idea?"

"None," he said. "Came out of left field for me. Tab is my best bud, and then to do something like this is just…" He shook his head, like a boxer who's received a vicious blow. "I tried to talk to him. But he said he couldn't. It wasn't the right time. Said it would mess up his process, just when he was going well. So like a coward I just snuck out of there."

"You didn't…"

"Kill him? Nah. Strange, isn't it? You would have thought I'd have been furious. But I was more disappointed for some reason. Disgusted. And then suddenly he turns up dead. Like divine intervention or something."

"You could have slipped out of the bar," said Chase. "Popped down into the studio, killed him, be back in minutes. No one would have noticed."

"Tony would have noticed. I can tell you that guy doesn't miss a trick." He grimaced. "No, I'm afraid you'll have to find your killer elsewhere, detective. Though now that you mention it, I am very disappointed that I never got the chance to have it out with Tab. I wanted him to tell me why, you know. Why he screwed over his best friend like that."

"So what's going to happen now?" asked Odelia.

"I don't know. Divorce? Separation?" He looked up, a pained look in his bleary eyes. "But I love my wife, you know. I don't want to lose her. Though I probably already have."

"Did the affair end or was it still going on?"

"According to Adima it had ended a couple of weeks ago. Which is probably the reason she had a breakdown and had to check into the center. Which is another score against me. Any decent husband would have noticed a thing like that, but like a jackass I didn't."

"Don't be too hard on yourself, Saul," said Odelia. "It's not your fault your wife had the affair. And of course you didn't know. They weren't going to advertise the fling, were they?"

He shrugged without looking up. "I've always known she liked him. Admired him. Heck, I admired him. But he should have kept his hands to himself. Then again, Tab always did take what he wanted. That's how he rolled. And the more successful he became, the more he thought he deserved everything he got and just wanted more of it. More money, more fame, more people admiring him and doing his bidding."

Odelia leaned in and rubbed the guy's back. Suddenly, before our eyes, he dissolved into desperate sobs. It was a distinctly sad scene, and somehow I just didn't see him as a killer. Then again, coming on the heels of the first shock, he might not have been himself when he went to confront his friend. And if Tab had simply dismissed him, he might have snapped and looped a piece of guitar string around the man's neck and pulled—hard.

"It's all right," Odelia murmured, and shared a look with her own husband.

"Poor guy," said Dooley. "He really loves his wife, doesn't he, Max?"

"Yeah, looks that way," I said.

"I'm starting not to like Tab anymore. He wasn't a very nice guy, was he?"

"No, he certainly is dropping a couple of notches in my esteem as well."

The man now dried his eyes. "I'm sorry," he said, "for going to pieces on you guys like this. It's just that—it's still all very raw, you know. I only found out yesterday, and then suddenly Tab goes and dies on us like this. It's all too much to take in."

"Have you been in touch with your wife, Saul?" asked Odelia.

"No, I haven't been taking her calls. I need some time for myself now before I talk to her again. I'm afraid if I hear her voice I'm just going to snap completely, you know."

Odelia nodded, and even Chase looked thoroughly sympathetic with the guy's ordeal. "Just let us know if there's anything you need," said the hardened cop.

"Is there anyone who can be with you?" asked Odelia.

"I've been talking to Darnell a lot. He's a good friend."

Not such a good friend that he didn't reveal Saul's big secret to the cops. But then Darnell had been under a lot of pressure himself lately. And somehow I had the impression more skeletons were about to fall from the late singer's closet.

CHAPTER 21

Chase and Odelia decided to have another chat with Madison Fitch, possibly to feel her out about some of the stuff they'd discovered since their earlier talk yesterday.

Tab's widow had agreed to meet up with us in the big house, and when we entered the living room it was clear that a pop legend had lived there. Large Warholesque portraits of the man himself decorated the walls, and the floor was of a checkerboard design that reminded me of a video clip of one of Tab's early hits. There was a big white grand piano parked in a corner of the room, and the couches looked a nice white leather. Exactly the kind of leather I like to dig my claws into.

It wasn't to be, though, for one look from Madison relegated us firmly to the floor.

"So what was it you wanted to see me about?" asked the woman, who was dressed in a tasteful black pantsuit today, as behooves a recent widow. "Have you found out who killed my husband?"

"We're still processing the information we've collected,"

said Chase noncommittally, "but we have one or two things we'd like to talk to you about."

"One of which is that your husband had abandoned the film project Darnell had been working on," said Odelia.

"Yes, Tab told me about that. Said he didn't feel comfortable sharing so much personal information with the public. At least not at this point in his career. Said he preferred to remain more of a mystery. He thought it would work wonders for his popularity."

"To remain a mystery?"

She made an idle gesture with her hand. "Some theory he had. Most artists overshare. Post about every little thing that happens in their lives. What they had for breakfast. Their latest haircut. Trips to the mall. Close-ups of their psoriasis flaring up. Prostate exam. Everything. But he felt that doing exactly the opposite might be the better strategy. Make people wonder. Be the man of mystery. That way they'd be more eager to latch onto whatever little snippet of information they could get—like his new album."

"We talked to Darnell, and he was pretty upset about the scrapping of his project."

"Yeah, I know. He's been working on it for years, and now all of a sudden Tab decided to cancel. But like I told him, we can always revisit the project at some point in the future. It's not that Tab didn't want to use the footage Darnell shot. He just didn't want to use it now."

"Do you think Darnell is capable of…"

"Murder?" She drew a tiny wrinkle in her brow. "I don't know. They say that we're all capable of murder, given the right circumstances, so…" But then she shook her head. "Not Darnell. He's always been very close to Tab, and just because of this misunderstanding doesn't mean he'd murder him."

But I couldn't help but notice that she didn't look entirely convinced.

"There is one other thing we need to talk to you about, Madison," said Chase, darting a look to his wife. "It's a little delicate, I'm afraid."

"Oh?" She looked at the detecting pair expectantly. "What is it?"

"I don't know if you're aware of this," said Odelia, "but Tab was having an affair… with Saul's wife Adima."

Madison blinked twice, then swallowed. "No," she said finally. "I didn't know that."

"By all accounts the affair had ended, but it had been going on for a while."

Madison nodded slowly, then glanced up at the large Warhol-style portrait of her husband. "No, this is news to me," she said softly. "So Adima, huh? How… odd."

"Odd, why?" asked Odelia.

"Because Tab once told me he didn't even like Adima. Said he didn't think she was the right partner for Saul. Too… plain. Too ordinary. Too vulgar, mostly. And yet," she added quietly. "And yet…"

"So you never knew about the affair? Never suspected anything?"

The widow was shaking her head slowly. "No, I did not. If I had, I'd probably… Well, I don't know what I would have done, but I certainly would have something to say about it."

"There's also Xanthe Bergson," said Odelia, now looking thoroughly uncomfortable but trudging on regardless. These things needed to be said, unfortunately.

"Oh, that's right. Xanthe and Rasheed. I've put them up at The Cedars for now."

"They're here?" asked Chase sharply.

"Yes, apparently they had some trouble at the hotel where they were staying, and they arrived here late last night, looking for a place to stay. So I gladly offered them a room.

We've got plenty of space, and they are big fans of my husband's work. So why not?"

"You are aware they were caught trying to sneak in here yesterday?"

"I know. But they're honeymooners. I decided to cut them some slack. It's been a difficult twenty-four hours for all of us, and it's the least I could do."

Odelia and Chase shared another quick look, then Odelia took a breath and said, "Xanthe claims that she and Tab enjoyed a one-night stand a couple of years ago."

Madison frowned. "A one-night stand."

"Yeah. She won a backstage pass in a radio station competition and when she met Tab after the show they hit it off and he invited her back to his hotel where they spent the night."

"When was this, do you know?"

"Three years ago."

Madison rubbed her face with her hands. "God, this just keeps getting worse and worse, doesn't it? So Tab had a one-night stand with a groupie and he had an affair with his best friend's wife. And now of course you're wondering why I didn't know that my husband was some kind of cheating… jerk? Well, I can assure you that I didn't know about any of this. What does that make me? An idiot? A fool? Too naive for my own good?"

"It makes you a trusting and loving wife whose husband took advantage of her trust," said Odelia gently.

Madison had folded her hands in her lap and stared down at that checkerboard floor, which frankly was already giving me a headache just by lying on it. "I don't know about all these affairs," she said finally. "But I do know that he loved me. A lot. So maybe it didn't count? Maybe this is what you get when you marry a pop star? Rock star? Any star?"

"He probably was subjected to a lot of temptation," said Odelia.

"Oh, of course. Women practically threw themselves at his feet. Any tour he did he had his pick, but he swore that he was never unfaithful. And he always came back to me. And I didn't want to be the kind of partner who checked his phone, looked through his emails, or even hired a private detective to keep tabs on him, you know. That would have driven me crazy. So I just didn't. I decided, when we got married, to trust him, and I always have."

"If there were two other women in his life," said Chase, "chances are that—"

"There were probably more," said Madison, giving the detective a level look. She smiled a tight smile. "I think it's a safe bet that there are. But what does it matter now? He's dead. So I'm not going to waste time torturing myself. Unless you think one of these women killed him?"

"That's not the assumption we're working from," said Chase.

"So what is the assumption?"

Chase spread his arms. "We're keeping our options open."

She smiled. "Then so am I."

"Are you going to show the Bergsons the door now?" asked Odelia.

Madison thought for a moment, then shrugged. "What's the point? No, I think I'll let them stay."

Chase rose to his feet, and so we all did. And we'd just said our goodbyes when suddenly there was a commotion in the hallway. Saul entered, looking flustered. "There's a woman here who wants to see you," he said apologetically. "And she won't take no for an answer."

He stepped aside, and we found ourselves looking at Deana Whisker, Ray Whisker's teenage sister, and she didn't look happy.

CHAPTER 22

Chase had decided to deflect Deana, figuring Madison already had enough on her plate and didn't need another shock. So first they were going to listen to what the girl had to say and then decide whether it was okay for them to relay the message to Tab's widow.

We were out in the garden, which had been created by a local landscape artist and which looked absolutely amazing. There were plenty of perennials and hedges providing privacy, but also wonderfully colorful flowers that smelled delicious.

"Don't eat them, Max," Dooley warned when he saw me study the flowers. "Remember the candy."

"Flowers aren't candy, Dooley," I said. "I'd never eat them." Or candy, for that matter.

"No, but I saw the way you were looking at them. Like you look at a bowl of kibble."

"I was simply admiring them," I said. "They're so colorful and they smell so nice."

"They're probably poisonous," he said, giving them a look of keen suspicion.

I decided to ignore his concerns and settled in on the smooth lawn, very near where Chase and Odelia had settled in with the Whisker girl. I even took a nibble at the grass, and thought it tasted even better than the grass at home. Yes, cats do eat grass from time to time. It works wonders for our digestion, if you must know.

"So what brings you here today, Deana?" asked Odelia.

The girl was dressed in ripped jeans and a pink angora sweater, her blond hair styled into feathery tresses. "Mom and dad sent me," she said. "They thought I might have more luck pleading our cause because I'm part of Tab's target audience." She grimaced. "I don't know what they're thinking. Or maybe they're not thinking at all. They're desperate is what they are. But then we're all desperate, I guess."

"Desperate? About what?"

"The hospital called this morning, wanting to know why the check bounced."

"What check?" asked Chase.

"The check Tab gave us."

"I didn't know they gave actual checks in those television shows," said Odelia.

"Oh, no, that giant cardboard they gave us wasn't an actual check, but later on he gave us a real check, so we could give it to the hospital to start the treatment. Only now it turns out the check wasn't valid or something, and when Mom and Dad called the compound this morning, Madison said she'd never heard about us, and referred us to a lawyer. And the lawyer said that he'd never heard about us either, and the upshot is that now it looks as if the whole thing was just a publicity stunt." When we all stared at her, she added, "For Tab's new album? His lawyer, who turned out to be a really nice guy, said that people like Tab pull these stunts all the time. They like to see their names attached to good causes, but when push comes to shove they don't actually like to fork over all of that money."

"So… your brother isn't going to get his treatment?" asked Odelia, clearly aghast.

Deana shook her head. "Looks that way. Pretty rotten thing to do, don't you think? We were really counting on that money. Without it, there won't be any treatment. Those hospitals aren't charities. They don't like to give you expensive drugs out of the goodness of their hearts. They need cold hard cash or they tell you to take a hike." She shrugged. "So looks like they told us to take a hike now. And so did Tab frickin' Fitch. And to think I downloaded all of his stupid songs and have been listening to them, like, nonstop."

"We'll talk to Madison," Odelia promised. "I'm sure something can be arranged."

"Yeah, ask her if she's got two million dollars lying around," the girl murmured, closing her eyes and briefly enjoying the feel of the sun on her eyelids. "Though she probably has. Only she won't want to part with it, will she? Those kind of people never do."

Chase's expression hardened, then he abruptly got up. "Let's go," he grunted.

The girl opened her eyes. "Where are we going?"

"We're going to talk to Madison, to tell her what her shit of a husband has been up to."

Deana smiled. "That's ten cents in the swear jar, Mr. Kingsley."

"I'd make it two million if I could," said Chase huskily.

True to his word, Chase actually did take Deana to see Madison, and when she heard what the girl had to say, she was as shocked as we all were. After a lengthy phone call with the same lawyer the Whiskers had talked to that morning, she quickly made up her mind. The upshot was that she invited the Whisker family to come and stay at the compound, as Tab had initially promised but hadn't bothered to back up with an actual invitation, and said she'd arrange everything: the treatment, the hospital stay for the rest of the family, and any aftercare Ray would need. It was the least she could do, she said, and I could tell she was starting to wonder how many more of Tab's surprises would be sprung on her.

When it was finally time for us to take our leave, we passed the Whisker family pulling up as we pulled out. They seemed quietly relieved, and I didn't wonder. I just hoped that at least Madison would be true to her word. But somehow I had a feeling she would.

"I wonder what else Tab forgot to mention to his wife," said Dooley as we traveled back to Hampton Cove. "Maybe there are more girlfriends? More sick kids he forgot?"

"He was a man with many secrets, that's for sure," I said. "And the more secrets, the more suspects for his murder." Which didn't make our investigation any easier.

I briefly pondered Harriet's words from the night before. There was going to be a big surprise in my life today, and it was going to make me glad about some of the choices I'd made. Could the surprise be Tab Fitch's complete lack of scruples? But how did that make me feel about my life choices? Then I dismissed the thought. What was I doing? Giving credence to a lot of nonsense someone in some office had made up? Nuts.

CHAPTER 23

"Okay, so what have we got? Fill me in, team," said Uncle Alec, leaning back in his chair until it creaked dangerously. One of these days it was going to break and the Chief would be lying on his ass on the floor. Luckily today was not that day.

"Plenty of suspects, plenty of motives for murder, Chief," said Chase, checking his notebook.

We were in the big man's office, Odelia and Chase bringing him up to date on the state of the investigation so far. Which to be absolutely honest was absolutely nowhere yet.

"Suspects. Give it to me," the Chief said, closing his eyes in utter concentration. I noticed his face had a reddish tinge, and assumed he'd spent the weekend in the backyard with his girlfriend the Mayor, taking in some sun and doing a bit of barbecuing, which he loved.

"So we've got the wife," said Chase, "who was on her way home when it happened, though technically she could have done it. Motive? Not much to go on. Her husband was having an affair, but she claims she didn't know about it."

"I don't think she did," Odelia supplied. "Hard to fake that look of surprise."

"Agreed," said Chase. "And also, she seemed genuinely fond of her husband."

"Wife Madison," the Chief grunted. "Opportunity, no motive. Go on."

"Then there's Xanthe and Rasheed Bergson."

"Who are they?"

"Honeymooners," said Odelia with a smile. "She's a big fan of Tab. Had a one-night stand with the man three years ago, convinced Rasheed to visit Fitchville for their honeymoon, though he didn't exactly look over the moon about it," she quipped, earning herself twin smiles from her husband and uncle.

"Motive?" asked the Chief.

"For her?" said Chase. "Could be that she felt jilted after the one-night stand. And as far as Rasheed is concerned, if he knew about his wife's fling he could have been out for revenge."

"Did he know?"

"He claims not to have known, but impossible to be sure."

"I don't think Xanthe is a suspect, though," said Odelia. "She's too much of a fan. And being jilted? I think she understood full well this was just a one-time deal."

"Agreed," said Chase with a nod. "Moving on, there's Saul Goff, Tab's childhood friend, whose wife confessed yesterday morning that she had an affair with Tab. She decided to come clean as part of her twelve-step program. She's in rehab," he clarified for the Chief's benefit.

The big man nodded. "Best friend's wife having an affair. Sounds like an excellent motive for murder. Alibi?"

"He was in the bar all morning, drinking away his sorrow, but he must have slipped out at some point to go to the bathroom. You can't drink that much alcohol and not have to get rid of some of that excess fluid. I checked the toilets, and it's easy to sneak out the back, then up to the house, into the basement where the studio is located, murder Tab, and sneak right back. I timed it, sir, and it took me all of ten minutes."

"Ten-minute toilet break. What did the bartender say?"

"He said he hadn't kept an eye on the guy all morning, and agreed that he could have been gone for as much as ten minutes without him noticing."

"Great. Motive, opportunity, means. I like him for this. Next?"

"Um, that would be Darnell Fitch."

"Fitch? Any relation?"

"Tab's cousin on his dad's side. Documentary maker who's been working on a film about his famous cousin for years. Until Tab decided to bury the entire project."

Uncle Alec opened his eyes and sucked in his breath through his teeth. "That must have hurt."

"It did. He felt betrayed, angry, you name it. And he was there. Confessed that he and Tab got into a big fight that morning. In fact Madison saw him leave the house just when she arrived back from her visit to the doctor. This would have been at one o'clock. Darnell says he didn't kill his cousin, and stepped out to cool off."

"Put him on top of the list," said Uncle Alec with a nod.

"And then there's Steve Rovira."

"Who's he?"

"A producer who worked with Tab on his first two albums. Tab screwed him out of a co-writing credit and the thing is probably heading to the courts at some point. He's staying at the Star and claims he spent the morning alone in his room. No one can vouch for him, and he definitely benefits from Tab's death, since Madison is bound to be more amenable to his claim than her husband."

"God, you weren't lying. There's more suspects here than dead sausages on Tex's grill when he's going well. Next?"

"That would be Dunton Plontek," said Odelia, picking up the baton from her husband. "He's the neighbor who protested against turning the countryside into a rock village. He accepted an offer to sell his farm this morning, for twice the market value, a price he would never have gotten from Tab, who was only willing to go up to twenty percent."

"Dunton Plontek," said Uncle Alec, "is he the guy with the bulldozer this morning?"

"That's him."

"Nice negotiation technique," the Chief grunted unhappily.

"And then there's the Whiskers," said Odelia.

Uncle Alec darted a glance down to me and Dooley. "Whiskers?" he asked with a frown.

"Yeah, Ray Whisker is a six-year-old boy with spinal muscular atrophy. He needs an expensive drug that Tab had promised to pay for, but turns out that he wasn't going to keep his promise, causing the kid to face an uncertain future. Now that Tab is dead they talked to the widow, and she's agreed to pay for the drug and also the aftercare."

"Alibis?"

"The family was supposed to stay up at the compound, but Tab reneged on his promise, so they were at the Star, hoping to receive some good news from Fitchville. They're each other's alibi."

"So the dad could have driven out to the compound, gotten into an argument with Tab about his little boy and broken promises and lost his temper," said the Chief, nodding.

"And then finally we have a sad case," said Chase. "I don't know if you remember Pino Seeds, Chief?"

"Pino Seeds," said his boss. "Where are the days? I didn't know he was still alive?"

"He is, though only barely. He fell out of a third-story window at the Star but he seems to be doing fine."

"Fell or was pushed?"

"Fell. I talked to him at the hospital and he said he lost his balance."

"So what's his story?"

"He was instrumental in securing Tab a record deal, until Tab's success eclipsed that of his mentor and he offered Pino to be his supporting act on his upcoming tour, which Pino refused as a lousy proposition."

"I don't blame him," Uncle Alec grumbled. "Pino is a legend."

"Legend or not, he's not as successful as he used to be, and he was feeling humiliated by his former protégé, as he wasn't shy about expressing on his Facebook page."

"Okay, so where was he when Tab was killed?"

"In the bar of the Star, downing one G&T after another. And even though I hate to say it, it looks as if this bartender did keep a close eye on him, though of course you never know."

"I think he's the least likely to have killed Tab," said Odelia. "He just doesn't seem physically strong enough to have garroted him. It takes considerable strength to kill a person that way."

"Yes, it does," said Uncle Alec, tapping a pencil on his desk and glancing down at the list of names his deputy had jotted down. "So who did it, people? Or are you telling me you think that any one of them could have killed Tab Fitch." When two sheepish faces stared back at him, he let out a curse. "Great. So we've got us another one of those, huh?"

"Looks like it, Chief," said Odelia. "Plenty of suspects but no physical evidence whatsoever."

"No fingerprints, shoeprints, DNA evidence, witness statements, nothing?"

Both Odelia and Chase shook their heads. "Nope," said Chase finally. "Zip."

He stared down at me for some reason. "I hate to say this, but what about pets? No cats, dogs, parrots, goats, pet snakes or pet tigers around at this Fitchville place?"

"Tab and Madison kept no pets," said Odelia.

"Plenty of people," I clarified, "but no pets."

"Mr. Plontek does have a cow," said Dooley.

"Yeah, but Bella didn't see anything," I added.

"Bella didn't see anything," Odelia translated dutifully.

"Who's Bella?" asked Uncle Alec.

"Dunton Plontek's cow."

"Christ," said the Chief, shaking his three chins in dismay. "Well, don't just sit there. Go out there and get me some results, people. Go on. Find me a killer and bring him to me!"

For a moment I thought he was going to say, 'Bring me his head on a platter,' but lucky for us he didn't. Besides, that kind of stuff is against the law these days, isn't it?

CHAPTER 24

That evening, dinner was on Marge and Tex, who had invited their daughter and Chase to enjoy some family time. And since Gran was still cruising the Norwegian fjords and Uncle Alec and Charlene had a gallery opening to attend, it was just the four of them, which suited them just fine. And I think everything would have been absolutely pleasant if Tex hadn't returned to the table at some point as the bearer of some bad news.

"I'm afraid the toilet is blocked again," he announced gloomily. "I've already called the plumber."

"You can use our toilet, Dad," said Odelia.

"Thanks, honey," said her father gratefully.

"So easy to have options, don't you think?" said Dooley. "Just like we have more than one litter box to do our business, so have our humans."

"Not litter boxes, though," said Harriet. "Humans don't like to do their business in a litter box. No idea why. It's plenty hygienic if you ask me."

"A water closet is a lot more practical," said Brutus. "All you have to do is flush, whereas we have to bury our business underneath a small pile of litter. Plus, someone has to clean out that litter at the end of the day, whereas humans simply flush it away."

"Yeah, they really seem to have the better deal," I said lazily. I'd eaten my fill, had done my business in my own litter box and now was prepared to take a long, pleasant nap.

"Can't you fix that toilet, Chase?" asked Marge, addressing her son-in-law. "Knowing that plumber, it's going to take days before he drops by, and all this time we'll have to use your toilet instead. And what are we going to do tonight and tomorrow night? I hate to do my business on a chamber pot. It's so impractical."

"I could take a look if you want," said Tex, but Marge ignored him. Clearly he wasn't the man for the job in her opinion.

"This would probably be the moment Gran gives us a lecture about how things used to be back in the day, when all they had was a chamber pot to use at night," said Odelia. She seemed more relaxed than before, when she and Chase had gone over the case and had come to the conclusion that they were nowhere near a solution yet. A nice meal had mellowed her out.

"It's probably some toilet paper that got stuck again," said Chase.

"You would think that when they rebuilt this place they put in decent plumbing," Marge said, looking unhappy. "But this is the third time that toilet has been blocked."

"It's probably nothing," said Odelia. "Like Chase says, some paper that got jammed."

"Yes, please, Chase," said Marge. "If you could take a look? That would be wonderful."

"Sure thing, Mom," said Chase, and got up to fulfill his promise.

"I want to see," said Dooley, also getting up. "I've never seen a toilet being unblocked."

"Oh, me too!" said Harriet. "I'm bored out of my skull here."

"No sign of a dark, handsome stranger today?" I quipped.

"No, and no brunette that is going to turn my world upside down either," said Brutus with a grin.

They both looked happy, now that Madame Burnett's dire predictions hadn't come to pass.

"And I, for one, haven't encountered any big surprises either," I said, yawning widely. I'd much rather have spent the rest of the evening on the couch, but since everyone was up and ready to see what Chase was up to, I didn't want to be the odd one out and so I joined the others up the stairs and into the bathroom.

The Pooles actually have two toilets: one regular one downstairs and a second one in the bathroom upstairs. The one downstairs has been out of commission for a week now, apparently missing some vital piece of the mechanism that will make it fully functional again, and so it was the one in the bathroom that earned itself Chase's special attention.

"Let's see what we've got," the cop murmured as he opened the lid and took a gander.

What I immediately noticed was the powerful stench that emanated from the device. Clearly Tex had done his business before realizing that he probably shouldn't have. It's happened to all of us, of course. Nature calls, and its call is hard to ignore. Like the man said: when you have to go, you have to go, and clearly Tex had come and gone and now it was up to Chase to deal with the aftermath.

"Let's give this a try," Chase said as he took a firm grip on a strange contraption located next to the toilet bowl. It was a rubbery thing with a wooden stick attached to it, and as he plunged it into the toilet, a sort of squelchy sound could be heard as Odelia's husband worked away at the odiferous obstruction. He sort of pumped his arm like a piston, his facial expression revealing his full focus on the task at hand, the tip of his tongue visible and droplets of sweat beading his furrowed brow.

"What is he doing, Max?" asked Dooley.

"It looks as if he's trying to suck out the obstruction," I said, studying the man's movements closely.

Humans have always been a particularly interesting breed for me. The things they do, and the reasons they do it for have never stopped exacting a powerful fascination. And this behavior on the part of the police detective was certainly gripping and extremely dramatic in nature. Chase reminded me of prehistoric man hunting and killing a wild beast, the way he now attacked that toilet with extreme determination and skill.

"Who do you think will win the battle?" asked Brutus. "Chase or that toilet?"

"Chase definitely has the edge," said Harriet, sounding like an ESPN commentator. "He's promised Marge he'd get results and results is exactly what he's going to get."

"He can't let her down," Brutus agreed. "He needs this to work or lose face."

"Plus he's in great shape here," Harriet continued. "Look at that focus, that sheer concentration. And the incredible strength and willpower he brings to the table."

"Yeah, that toilet doesn't stand a chance against an all-rounder like Chase."

"Chase Kingsley truly is a man on a mission. The right guy for the job."

They were right. Chase was plunging like a man on fire, his brawny arm yanking away like nobody's business. Finally he paused and wiped his sweat with the back of his hand.

"I think that did it," he declared, looking relieved. "Let's give this a try, fellas."

I watched his hand move to the lever that activates the toilet's flushing mechanism, and for some reason a sudden sense of foreboding swept through me. My tummy roiling, I called out, "Chase, no!" But of course it was too late. Plus, he couldn't understand me.

And before our very eyes, suddenly that toilet seemed to explode: a geyser of water sprung forth, spraying a kind of brown liquid all over the ceiling, the walls and… us!

When the fountain had finally spent its powerful excretion, we were all covered in Tex's latest bowel movement: me, Dooley, Harriet, Brutus, and of course Chase. And since the latter had been standing over the toilet, he'd actually borne the brunt of the emission. The man was simply covered in the stuff from top to toe: his face, his hair, his clothes…

"Look, Harriet," said Dooley. "There's your dark, handsome stranger. It's Chase!"

"Yeah, and your brunette is on top of his head, Brutus," I said.

"She definitely rocked my world," Brutus grumbled unhappily.

"Can you please be quiet," Harriet lamented. "This isn't the time for toilet humor."

I would have said there had never been a better time for toilet humor, but then who am I? In spite of our predicament, Dooley and I shared a grin. Looked like Madame Burnett's predictions had come true, after all. I'd even experienced my big surprise, and it had certainly made me happy about some of the choices I'd made. Namely to live in Odelia's house and not in Marge and Tex's, with their wonky toilets!

"Babe!" suddenly Odelia's voice sounded from the door. "What happened?"

"Do you have to ask?" Chase said. "The toilet exploded, that's what happened."

Tex and Marge had now also appeared in the door, attracted by the noise, and they had a hard time containing their glee, as had Odelia. In fact the only one who wasn't laughing was Chase, but then I think he could be excused for not seeing the funny side.

"Better take a shower," Marge suggested.

"Well, at least you managed to unblock the toilet," said Tex. "So good job, buddy."

"Thanks… Dad," said Chase, and stepped, fully clothed, into the shower.

And since the four of us were in much the same state as Chase, Odelia then took us into that shower, too, and for the next ten minutes we were all subjected to the powerful spray of that most hideous and nefarious invention ever made by man: the showerhead!

"I hate Madame Burnett," said Harriet when Marge was toweling her dry. "Hate her!"

"Me, too," said Brutus gloomily as he was subjected to the same treatment.

"At least there was no candy," said Dooley. "That would have been the worst."

It took our humans three hours to clean that bathroom, and even when all was said and done, it still had a funny smell and the ceiling needed a new coat of paint. The episode made me appreciate my litter box all the more. It might not be the best solution for the disposal of feline waste, but at least a litter box will never attack you the way this treacherous toilet had. Something to consider next time you visit a Bed Bath & Beyond.

CHAPTER 25

When a detective is completely stuck, as sometimes happens, you'll often see that they start to go over the same ground they've already covered at an earlier stage in their investigation, in the hope of unearthing some new piece of evidence. And so it was that the day after Uncle Alec had enjoined Chase and Odelia to bring him Tab's killer, they repaired to Fitchville once more, to talk to the same people they'd already talked to: Madison, Saul Goff, Darnell... They even had another chat with Dunton Plontek. All to no avail, of course, since they'd already given their statements and had nothing more to add.

Dooley and I soon bored of the endless interviews, and started roaming the place that Tab had built for himself. It was a pretty impressive accomplishment, of course, and must have cost the man a pretty penny. But then Tab was a multimillionaire, and like many multimillionaires before him, had decided to invest in real estate, always a sound plan.

"Must be nice to live in a place like this," said Dooley. "Though it's a little big for my taste." We'd finished roaming the grounds behind the houses, and were now returning to the compound itself. "I'll bet you can spend days out here and never meet a living soul."

"It's big but it's not that big, Dooley," I said.

"But it is, Max. A lot of couples have separate bedrooms, but Tab and Madison could have taken separate houses. And then changed houses every week if they'd wanted to."

"Yeah, I guess they could have."

"What I don't understand is why, Max. Why does one person need half a dozen different houses to live in. Who needs that much space?"

"Which is probably why Madison is going to turn Fitchville into a convention center," I said. "Or even an orphanage or a homeless center." Fitchville had been Tab's dream, and now that he was gone, Madison didn't know what to do with it. It certainly was too big for her, and to sell it all off seemed like a bad idea. The notion of giving something back to the community had stuck with her, though, and she was considering different future solutions for the compound.

We'd drifted back to The Cedars, which was being used as a guest house. We decided to take a peek, our natural curiosity leading us to inspect the different rooms. Saul was staying there, and so were Darnell and Steve Rovira. All of them had been awarded their own sets of suites, which were spacious and luxuriously appointed. The Whisker family was a new addition, of course, and also the Bergsons had found a temporary home there on the premises, finally enjoying their honeymoon in style. The couple seemed to have reconciled, and were back together, their divorce plans on hold.

And it was in their suite that we suddenly found ourselves, curious to discover how they'd settled in. Dooley, of course, was still adamant that they were our prime suspects, and in a bid to humor him, I decided to take a sniff around to see what we could find.

There wasn't all that much in the form of personal possessions, since the couple was essentially backpacking: there was some luggage on the floor, some clothes in the closets, and some personal items in the bathroom. But apart from that the rooms that constituted the suite looked as pristine as they had been before Xanthe and Rasheed moved in.

Plenty of the same kinds of Warhol-style portraits adorned the walls, something Xanthe would probably love and Rasheed wouldn't, and I was just about to abandon our impromptu search when suddenly a familiar scent filled my nostrils and an even more familiar sensation tickled my spine. It made my tail distend of its own accord, and I knew we'd hit upon something.

"What is it, Max?" asked Dooley, who'd noticed the change in my demeanor. "Is it candy? Have you found her bag of candy? Don't touch it, Max. It's probably poisoned."

"Not candy," I murmured as I sniffed the air near the closet where the smell had first filled my nostrils and tickled my spidey senses. "Something else. Something more interesting..." I slipped into the closet, picking up the woodsy scent mixed with glue—a clear sign this closet was still relatively new and unused. But there was something else mixed in with the newness. It smelled a lot like... blood. Human blood.

I stuck my nose between two towels then, and there it was: a piece of string.

"Dooley," I said. "I think I've found the murder weapon, buddy."

"The murder weapon!" my friend cried. "Back away slowly, Max."

"It's all right. It's just a piece of string, but if I'm not mistaken, there's blood on it."

"Blood!"

Which would stand to reason, of course, if it really was the murder weapon.

Just then, the door to the suite opened and I looked up in alarm. But before I could crawl out of that closet, footsteps approached, and when I took a peek through the crack in the door, I saw that none other than Saul Goff was stealthily approaching, looking here and there, not unlike the way Dooley and I had entered the suite only minutes before.

The man was wearing sneakers, making sure to tread carefully and silently. When he spotted the Bergsons' luggage on the floor he immediately started rifling through it.

Dooley had hidden under the bed the moment Tab's childhood friend had walked in, and was now darting anxious glances in my direction. What was this guy doing here?

And I'd just mouthed for Dooley to stay where he was, when suddenly I locked eyes with Mr. Goff, and I froze. Dang! I'd let myself be caught! Worst part: I was stuck!

"Hey, kitty cat," said the sinewy guy, and bent down next to me. "What are you doing here, huh?"

"I could ask you the same thing," I said stiffishly.

"Are you hungry? Are you looking for food?"

Why is it that humans always assume that cats are looking for food? It's stigmatizing.

"I don't have anything to give you, kitty cat," said Saul. "But I'm sure…" He paused as he stared past me into the closet. "Wait a minute," he said. "What have we here?"

And then he reached past me, lifted the towel and whistled through his teeth.

"Holy moly," he said softly. "Is that what I think it is?"

"It certainly is, buddy," I said. "Don't touch it, will you? That's evidence."

But instead of touching it, he took out his phone and dialed a number.

"Police? Yes, I think I've found important evidence in a murder case. Thank you." He waited a moment, then said,

"Hi, this is Saul Goff. I think I've found what looks like the weapon that murdered Tab Fitch. I'm in the suite where the honeymooners are staying. Yes, detective. I'll stay right here. Please hurry. I don't know when they'll be back. No, I'm alone here right now." He darted a look down at me. "Except for a very fat orange cat."

CHAPTER 26

Look, I'm not one of those cats who always needs to be in the limelight. I'm not an attention seeker. But I do feel that the credit should be given where the credit is due. And the fact of the matter was that I found that piece of string, not this annoying human who goes around hurling insults at innocent cats like me. Now he was gallivanting all over the place claiming to have solved his friend's murder—though if he were honest he would be the first to admit Tab was a lousy friend—and calling me not only fat but also orange!

I'd told Odelia the moment she arrived that I found that piece of guitar string, and of course she believed me, but who cares about the truth? No one!

At least Xanthe and Rasheed Bergson were duly placed under arrest on suspicion of the murder of Tab Fitch, and transferred to the station to be interrogated. The piece of string did indeed contain a little bit of blood, and also a ginger hair that might have belonged to the murdered singer, and currently the blood was being checked to see if it was a match for Tab's, which I had no doubt it was.

Odelia had taken us into the police station, and we were watching through the one-way mirror as Chase took a first stab at Xanthe, who had dissolved into a flood of tears.

"I didn't do it!" the blue-haired groupie announced to anyone who would listen. "I loved Tab! He was the only man I wanted to be with. I would have had his baby if he'd wanted me to. Why would I kill him? It makes no sense!"

"The murder weapon was found in your room, Xanthe," said Chase, placing a picture of the guitar string on the table in front of the accused. "So how do you explain that?"

She stared at the picture as she dabbed at her tears with the sleeve of her shirt. "I can't, but I would never hurt Tab. He knew how much I admired him." She glanced up at Chase, a look of hopelessness in her eyes. "You don't think… that Rasheed…"

"I thought you were together the whole time?"

"Yes, we were, except…" She wiped at her eyes some more. "We weren't."

"What do you mean, you weren't?"

She stared down at the picture some more, trying to wrap her mind around what was happening. "I wanted to pay a visit to Tab. Catch a glimpse of him, you know. I was hoping he'd remember me, and he'd call off his security people when he did. And then we'd have a chat, just like old times. Maybe even be together again. But I couldn't get over that fence. It was too high. So Rasheed said he'd look for another way in and told me to stay put. And so I did."

"How long was he gone for?"

"I don't know. Twenty minutes? Something like that."

"Plenty of time to find Tab," said Chase thoughtfully.

"But why would he kill Tab? He had no reason to."

"He might have found out that you slept with him."

"I only told him about that yesterday." She slumped. "I wish I never did. Things haven't been the same between us.

Rasheed insists he wants to divorce. But I don't want a divorce. I love him."

"Yesterday you told us you wanted a divorce. That you couldn't be with a man who didn't understand that Tab was the most important person in your life."

"Yeah, well, I changed my mind," said the girl, blowing a strand of blue hair from her face.

"So you think Rasheed might have known about you and Tab and decided to kill him?"

Xanthe shrugged. "It's possible. He's smart. He might have picked up on it somehow."

"Did you ever exchange messages with Tab? Chat on your phone?"

"No, never. I did write about it to Janice, though."

"Who's Janice?"

"My best friend."

Chase arched a meaningful eyebrow.

Xanthe's eyes went wide. "He read my emails!" She balled her hands into fists. "Of all the mean, rotten, dirty... He had no right. No right, I'm telling you!"

"Don't you think murdering a person is a lot worse than reading an email?"

Her lips moved wordlessly for a moment, as she came to terms with this horrible truth. "Rasheed killed Tab! There's no other explanation! He read in my emails about my affair with Tab and he decided to kill him!"

"I thought it was just a one-time thing?"

"It was, but I carried him in my heart always." She placed her hands on her heart, then formed a heart with her fingers. "I'll always love him. Always forever and ever and ever." Then her face crumpled like a used tissue. "And I *hate* Rasheed for what he did! I hate, hate, hate, *hate* him!"

"Oh, dear," said Odelia next to me. "She's very volatile, isn't she? Love, hate, love, hate."

"Yeah, I'm getting whiplash here," I said.

※

The next person to be led into the interview room was Rasheed. He didn't look too hot. Quiet and withdrawn, and that cut his wife had delivered him was red and swollen. Clearly it needed attention and a swab with an antibacterial.

"So this piece of string was found in your room," said Chase, placing the picture in front of the man. "The same piece of string that was used to kill Tab Fitch. What do you have to say about that, Rasheed?"

"Nothing," said the man quietly. "Except there must be some kind of mistake."

"You didn't put it there, is that what you're saying?"

"That's exactly what I'm saying. I didn't put it there and I've never seen it before."

"So how did it end up in your room?"

He shrugged. "How should I know?"

"Do you think Xanthe knew about it?"

He frowned. "Xanthe? What do you mean?"

"If you didn't put it there, she must have, right?"

He smiled a tired smile. "I don't think you understand, detective. My wife is crazy about Tab. She's always been crazy about him, only I never fully understood the depth of her affection for the guy. She confessed to me that she slept with him, and would have had his babies if he'd wanted to. *His* babies, you see, not mine. In fact only yesterday she told me she wants a divorce, since I don't appreciate the extent of her abiding love for Tab."

"So why did you accept Madison Fitch's invitation to stay at the compound?"

"Free lodging? Free food? A chance to see the famous

Fitchville? Why would I pass up an opportunity like that? And besides, the suite is big enough for the two of us."

"So you've been avoiding each other, is that it?"

"Like the plague," he said with a grimace as he leaned forward.

"Xanthe thinks you killed Tab."

He stared at the cop. "She said that?"

He nodded. "She says that when you arrived at the compound yesterday morning she couldn't scale the fence, so you went in search of another way in. She says you were gone maybe twenty minutes. Plenty of time to crawl over that fence, find Tab and kill him, wouldn't you say?"

"But I didn't! Yes, I tried to find a part of the fence where we could both climb over undetected, and eventually I found it and then went back to get Xanthe. It didn't matter in the end since we were caught anyway, so I never found Tab or killed him, like you suggest."

"So that's your story, is it?"

"It's not a story—it's the truth! Besides, I'd never been to the compound before. How would I even know where to find Tab? I read in the paper that he was killed in his recording studio, which was located underground. I didn't even know he had a studio."

"I guess you got lucky."

"Lucky! Why would I even want to kill Tab? I wasn't a fan of his music, but that's no reason to kill a person."

"He slept with your wife, Rasheed."

"I didn't know about that! I only found out yesterday when Xanthe told me."

"Are you sure? You didn't happen to read her emails?"

"Her emails? No, I didn't read her emails."

"Are you denying that you knew your wife wrote to Janice about Tab?"

"No, I knew about that, of course. But I never read those emails."

"Never felt curious to know what she wrote to her best friend?"

"No—yes, of course I was curious. But it was her personal stuff. It wasn't my business to snoop and…" He gave Chase a look of suspicion. "Did she tell you I read her emails?"

Chase nodded.

"Oh, God," said the young man, and squeezed his eyes shut in a gesture of extreme distress. "This is just great. So now my wife thinks I killed her favorite artist."

"Can I make one suggestion, Rasheed?"

"What?"

"Confess, son. Just get it off your chest. You'll feel much better when you do."

He rocketed up from his chair, which clattered to the floor. "But I didn't kill him!"

"What do you think, Max?" asked Dooley.

"I don't know," I said musingly. "If he didn't kill him, and she didn't kill him, then how did the murder weapon end up in their room?"

"Good question," said my friend.

Chase decided now was perhaps a good time to take a break, and walked out of the interview room. He took a seat at the edge of the table and rubbed his face. "Any news?"

"They searched the couple's flat in Queens," said Odelia, "but haven't found anything useful. Plenty of pictures of Tab, though, which must have annoyed Rasheed."

"Maybe that's why he killed him. Having to stare at pictures of the guy while you're married to his biggest fan must have been galling."

"Oh, and the results from the lab came back. It's confirmed: the blood on the wire is Tab's, and the wire is a string from his guitar. A perfect match, in fact. Looks like the killer snapped it off and then used it to strangle him."

"Strangled with his own guitar string. Now there's irony for you," Chase muttered as he stared bleakly at Rasheed, who had sunk down on his chair again and sat with his head on the table, looking pretty forlorn.

"If neither of the Bergsons killed him," said Odelia, "then we must assume that the actual killer planted that wire in their room, to try and frame them."

"Saul Goff, you think?"

"It was there before Saul arrived," I said.

"He could have planted it before you got there," said Odelia, "and then miraculously 'discovered' it where he himself placed it."

"Did he say anything about how he came to look for it in the Bergsons' room?" I asked.

"He said he was following a hunch," said Odelia.

"Saul?" asked Chase.

Odelia nodded.

"A hunch?" I said with a frown.

"Just like our hunch," Dooley clarified.

"I know, but still. It's a pretty long shot."

"Saul said he'd always had his suspicions about Xanthe," Odelia explained. "Said she was exactly the kind of crazy groupie he'd often warned Tab about. So when she entered the picture he says he knew she must have killed him."

"But why would Tab's self-proclaimed biggest fan want to kill him?"

Odelia shrugged. "Because she's deranged? Because she felt rejected? She did say she wanted to have the man's babies, so maybe when he turned her down she got mad?"

"But why wait three years?"

"It's not so easy to gain access to a star of Tab's caliber, Max. They're well-protected. So maybe this was her first chance to get close to him and so she took it. I mean, if what they're saying is true, then she was alone for twenty minutes, too. Plenty of time to find Tab and kill him."

"I don't know," said Chase. "Somehow it just doesn't add up, does it? The guy is right. How did either of them know where to find Tab?"

"Xanthe could have known," said Odelia. "An obsessed fan like her would have known everything about her biggest idol, including where he spent most of his time."

We all thought about this for a moment, and finally Dooley said, "See, Max? I told you the candy lady did it."

CHAPTER 27

We all decided to take a breather. Even though Uncle Alec was happy with the arrest, and was convinced that either Xanthe or Rasheed or both had killed Tab, the rest of us weren't as sanguine about the couple's guilt. And so they put the Bergsons on ice and went to have lunch.

Dooley and I, even though we could have joined them, decided to pay a visit to Kingman instead, and see if he couldn't provide us with some sustenance. Kingman's human, who runs the General Store, might have received another batch of fine kibble, and so it behooved us to sample it—all for the general good, of course.

As luck would have it, Kingman offered us a choice of two different kinds of delicious nuggets, and by the time we'd eaten our fill, I was frankly bursting at the seams.

"He called Max a fat orange cat," Dooley was telling Kingman, who had to laugh at this.

"You scratched him, of course," he said.

"No, I didn't scratch him, Kingman," I said. "What do you think I am? An animal?"

"You shouldn't let them get away with this," said our friend. "No one has the right to call you fat, Max. You're simply… fashionably chubby, that's all."

I gave him a nasty look, which he took in stride with a grin.

"We did catch a killer today," said Dooley. "Or even two."

"You did?"

"Oh, yes. The candy lady and her husband. Though it's not clear which one of them did it."

"Or neither," I muttered darkly. I'd stretched out next to Kingman and so did Dooley and for a few minutes we simply watched the world go by. From time to time one of Wilbur's customers would bend over and give us a tickle under the chin or a cuddle, and that was all right by me.

"Have you heard the latest?" said Kingman. "Rudolph's been arrested."

"Arrested? Why?"

Rudolph is Wilbur's brother, and he's been touring Eastern Europe with his death metal band Satan's Brood.

"The weirdest story, and typical Rudolph. The band is in Rumania right now, where apparently they're crazy about death metal, and he had gone into one of those internet cafés since his phone had gone and died on him. Only the guy before him had left his Gmail account open, and so Rudolph couldn't resist the temptation to take a peek at his emails. Turns out he was emailing back and forth with some other guy about getting together and hunting and murdering some poor innocent schmuck that weekend."

"Oh, no."

"Can you imagine? They were serial killers! So Rudolph immediately alerts the police, and thanks to him they catch the most notorious pair of killers the country's ever seen."

"Well, what do you know?" I said.

"I know, right? They called them the Buckle Bandits, on

account of the fact that they always left a buckle at the scene of the crime, strapped around their victims' neck."

"So why did they arrest Rudolph?" asked Dooley.

"They figured it was too much of a coincidence for him to hit upon these Buckle Bandits, especially since the police have been looking for them for years, so now they figure he must be involved somehow, especially since he looks like a serial killer himself and he's the lead singer of a band called Satan's Brood. So now he's locked up in some maximum-security hellhole in Bucharest trying to find a lawyer who'll represent him."

"He should talk to the American Embassy," I advised.

"He did, but they think he might be a serial killer, too!"

It certainly was quite a story, and one that could only happen to Wilbur's kooky brother. And as I ruminated on the elements of the unlikely event, suddenly something seemed to click into place in my head. Certain aspects of the Tab Fitch murder case. And before long, I was lost in thought, trying to fit everything together, as one does.

CHAPTER 28

We were all gathered in the big meeting room in the main house at Fitchville. Xanthe and Rasheed had been released from custody especially for the occasion, and all the others were there as well: Madison, Darnell Fitch, Saul Goff, Val Kip, Steve Rovira, Dunton Plontek, all of the Whiskers, and even Pino Seeds, who'd recovered from his tumble.

The only one who wasn't there was Madame Burnett, but then who needs her?

Odelia and Chase were doing the honors, and all of us were sitting in a circle, as if we were holding our own AA meeting, something Saul Goff's wife would have appreciated.

"I don't understand," said Dunton Plontek. His ruddy face looked even veinier than usual, and his coveralls even dirtier. Fortunately he hadn't brought Bella this time, but he had brought his foul mood. Which was surprising, since he was a very rich man now. "Why did you tell us to come here for this meeting? What's the big idea?"

"The big idea is to finally reveal to you who killed Tab

Fitch," said Odelia. "And to do that we want to take you through the case as it developed. All of you, at one point or another, were suspects, and so I think you'll find it interesting to know how we went about this investigation."

"We know who killed Tab," said Saul. "It was those two over there." He gestured with his head to Xanthe and Rasheed Bergson, who looked very unhappy to be there.

"Let's just hear them out, shall we?" Pino Seeds suggested. "I for one can't wait to find out what happened. And when we do, I hope there's drinks at the bar?" He cast a hopeful look in Madison's direction, who didn't respond, causing Pino to sag a little. He still had his arm in a sling, and the bruises on his face were a vivid purple, but at least he was alive.

"Okay, so when the case started it was unclear to us what a possible motive could have been to murder Tab," said Chase. "Madison, of course, stood to inherit her husband's possessions, both this compound and his royalties, but by all accounts they were a happy and united couple, so that seemed far-fetched."

Madison nodded once in acknowledgment.

"Saul was overheard arguing with Tab on the morning of the murder, and later was seen drinking at The Tab, for reasons that weren't clear to us at first. Darnell was seen stalking off, clearly angry about something, and of course there was the incident with Bella the cow, which you, Mr. Plontek, had managed to maneuver into Tab's pond."

"Pool," Dunton corrected the detective. "It's not a pond, it's a pool."

"Point taken," Chase said with a nod. "Also, you were seen leaving the compound around the time of the murder, which made you our suspect number one."

"Load of nonsense," the farmer grumbled.

"We soon found out that the fight between Tab and Saul

was about the fact that Saul's wife Adima had confessed to Saul that morning that she'd had an affair with Tab. An affair that had since ended."

"I would never kill Tab," Saul reiterated an earlier statement. "He was my best friend."

"He was also your wife's lover for months," Chase pointed out, causing Saul to glower at him. "And then of course there was Darnell, the documentary maker, spending years of his life following his cousin around with his camera, until Tab suddenly came out and told him one day that there would be no documentary. No lucrative Netflix deal. No career in filmmaking. No nothing. Years of hard work and dedication flushed down the drain."

"We might still revisit the work you did at a later date," Madison assured Darnell, who nodded absentmindedly.

"Suffice it to say that both Saul and Darnell had an excellent motive for murder," Chase continued, "not to mention that they were both there when it happened."

"I was at the bar," Saul reminded us.

"Yes, but you could have snuck out and done the deed. Which brings us to Steve." All attention turned to the pasty-faced producer. "Steve Rovira who was cheated out of his royalties for the songs he and Tab co-wrote. A decision that saw him lose millions."

"I was in my room at the hotel," Steve declared stubbornly.

"Where no one saw you," said Odelia.

"We also met the Bergsons, Xanthe and Rasheed," Chase continued, "who were here when Tab was killed, clambering over the fence. Xanthe had a one-night stand with Tab three years ago after a concert, and if Rasheed had found out about that, it would have given him an excellent reason to get rid of his love rival. As it happens, though, Rasheed only found out after the fact, and his only motive for murder would have been that he wasn't a big fan of Tab's music."

"I'm starting to like it a little," said Rasheed with a wan smile and a quick sideways glance to his wife, who ignored him.

"Xanthe pointed us in the direction of the Whiskers," said Chase, "a family cheated out of a life-saving two-million-dollar drug by Tab, who made a lot of promises he had no intention to keep, and also set us on the trail of Pino Seeds, an artist who acted as a mentor to Tab when he was just starting out, only to be stabbed in the back and humiliated by him."

"Hey, that's show business for you," said Pino, spreading his arms, then wincing.

"I must confess the solution eluded us for a long time," said Odelia. "But then Saul found the murder weapon in Xanthe and Rasheed's room, which put the investigation on track again."

"You found the murder weapon?" asked Darnell.

Saul nodded proudly. "Just following a hunch," he said.

"Of course now we know that the murder weapon was planted in that room," said Chase, "by the real killer, who also nudged Saul into taking a closer look at the Bergsons."

"Huh?" said Saul. "What do you mean?"

"Someone very skillfully put that 'hunch' in your head, Saul," said Odelia.

"No, it was my idea—all mine," he said, looking around, as if trying to convince the others.

"Who was it that put the idea in his head?" asked Carly Whisker, leaning in. She'd been following the back-and-forth with rapt attention, as we all had.

"We'll come to that," Chase assured her.

"It was *my* hunch," Saul insisted quietly.

"I think at this point we'd run out of leads to follow," said

Odelia honestly. "There were so many people who seemed to have a bone to pick with Tab, and plenty with no alibi, that it was hard to determine what had actually happened that fateful morning. What finally clinched it for us was the internet café."

They all looked up at this. "Internet café? Do they still exist?" asked Deana Whisker with a light laugh.

"Oh yes, they do," said Odelia. "And Xanthe paid a visit to one, didn't you, Xanthe?"

The blue-haired groupie nodded. "I ran out of data," she said. "Crappy provider."

"Xanthe walked into the internet café to check her email, only she forgot to log off when she finished," Chase picked up the thread. "So the person who came after her would have found the email she'd written open on the screen. And of course, human nature being what it is, this person read that email. And was shocked to find what it said."

"What did it say?" asked Pino Seeds curiously.

"Just some stuff about Tab," said Xanthe with a shrug.

"Xanthe had been writing to a friend about her date with Tab," said Odelia. "She said she hoped to meet Tab again and that he'd remember their night together. It also said something that Tab had revealed to her at the time." She paused for effect. "Tab insisted on using protection, not because of the risk of pregnancy, but because he had a thing about STDs. So when Xanthe told him that condoms sometimes break, he said that she had nothing to worry about, since he'd had the snip."

"The snip?" asked Deana Whisker, darting a confused look at her mom.

"Vasectomy," said her mother. "To make sure men can't have babies."

"Oh," said Deana. "So Tab couldn't have babies? But why?"

"Because he made a vow long ago that he never wanted to

have kids," said Saul. "Though honestly I didn't know he'd actually had the operation," he added with a glance to Madison, who sat stony-faced now.

"The person who read that email was you, wasn't it, Madison?" asked Odelia gently. "You discovered Tab's secret that morning, and it shocked you to the core. Because you and Tab had been trying for a baby for a long time, and he'd never even once mentioned that he couldn't have babies. He just let you think it was you."

"He had excellent volume and motility," said Madison automatically. "That's what Dr. Hoey said. Nothing wrong with him. So I just figured it was all because of me."

"But it wasn't, was it? He might have had excellent volume and motility, but that's because he turned in a sample that wasn't his."

A shocked silence followed this revelation.

"So… whose sample was it?" asked Val Kip.

"Mine," said Darnell, blinking confusedly. "Though I had no idea he was going to pass it off as his own, I swear." He gave Madison a pleading look, but she sat frozen in place. "He said the lab needed it to compare to his own sample. To make sure his own… stuff was up to snuff. Something about our DNA being the same because we were family. Honestly I didn't understand what he was going on about, and I didn't give it a lot of thought either."

"He needed your sample because his own sample would have proven that he couldn't have kids," said Odelia. "And then he'd have to confess to Madison that he'd lied to her all these years. Making her think it was her fault that they couldn't have a family."

"My god," Carly gasped, bringing a hand to her face. "The bastard."

Madison shook her head, then suddenly her carefully maintained composure collapsed and her face contorted into a mask of grief. "Tab told me we just had to keep trying. That eventually we'd get lucky. And all this time…" Her voice died away.

"You talked to him that morning, didn't you? Told him what you'd discovered. What did he say?"

"He said he never wanted to have kids. That he made a vow a long time ago as a young man but that he didn't want to lose me so he hadn't told me about the operation. That he hoped I'd finally give up and that it would be just the two of us, no kids. So he just let me live in hope only to see it crushed over and over again and didn't even bother to tell me the truth. That it wasn't me but him. That he was incapable of having a baby. Didn't even want a baby." She bent forward, tears dripping from her eyes onto the floor. "It was the worst thing he could have done to me. The absolute worst betrayal imaginable. I'd always known he had a selfish streak, but this was… He knew I wanted to have a baby. That it was my deepest wish to start a family. I'd told him from the beginning. He knew. And still…"

"So you killed him," said Odelia softly.

Madison nodded. "One of his guitar strings had snapped. It seemed more important to him than our conversation. He kept fiddling with it, telling me the baby thing was no big deal. That babies were just a hindrance. That they would slow him down on his road to success. That I shouldn't be so selfish and only think about my own happiness." She took a big, gulping breath, then said on a sob, "So I finally just snatched that damn string from his hands and wrapped it around his neck and pulled as hard as I could."

A deafening silence followed these words, then suddenly Carly Whisker got up from her chair and walked over to where Madison sat and wrapped her arms around her. It was a touching moment, and as Madison dissolved into tears, I think there was a lot of surprise at this turn of events in that room, but also a lot of compassion.

Finally, Xanthe murmured, "I don't think I'm a fan of Tab anymore."

Next to her, Rasheed released a sigh of relief. "Well, hallelujah!"

CHAPTER 29

"It was a tough one, this case," I said. "But we finally did it."

"You did it, you mean," said Brutus, and yawned.

"We all did. Team effort."

I eyed Odelia and Chase, seated at the table in Marge and Tex's backyard, and enjoying a well-deserved family meal. Uncle Alec looked pleased as punch, as he always does when we've managed to put a tough case to bed—and of course the food that was being served didn't hurt. He was actually busy sliding a large greasy sausage into his mouth, until he caught sight of his girlfriend's disapproving eye and slid it out again, then put it down and sliced off a tiny piece. Much better, Charlene's expression seemed to say.

Gran still hadn't returned from her Norwegian cruise, but had sent a message that she was alive and well and that Scarlett had managed to seduce the captain of the ship and she wasn't happy about it, because it meant she was having to go on trips all by herself.

"How did you know it was Madison?" asked Harriet.

"A combination of things, actually," I said. "The fact that

I'd seen her enter the internet café after Xanthe, for one, Rudolph Vickery reading a serial killer's message on a computer in a Rumanian internet café, and the fact that we met Madison at the gynecologist's office that morning looking pale and nervous and not at all herself. Plus the fact that Xanthe mentioned something about Tab insisting on using protection against STDs—not pregnancy but STDs… I don't know. It just sparked this idea in my head."

"Did it hurt, Max?" asked Dooley. "When you felt this spark?"

I smiled at my friend and patted him on the back. "Didn't hurt one bit, buddy."

"Oh, good. You had me worried there for a second."

"So when I told Odelia about this idea that Madison might have read one of Xanthe's emails, she went to the internet café and checked their CCTV. Turns out that Madison had indeed sat at the same computer Xanthe had left just before, reading something that was on there very intently, sitting perfectly still for a long time. The person at the counter remembers that Madison had turned white as a sheet. She even asked her if everything was all right. She thought she was going to faint. And then of course Odelia and Chase interviewed Xanthe again, and she confirmed that Tab told her about the vasectomy."

"Why didn't she tell you before?" asked Harriet.

"She didn't think it was important. She just figured everyone knew."

"Not only did nobody know, Madison didn't know," said Brutus.

"Poor woman," said Harriet. "I really feel for her, you know."

"Yeah, we all do," I said. "And I'm sure the jury will take what Tab did to her into account when they come back with their verdict."

"Odd that Tab never told his best friend, but he did tell some random groupie," said Brutus.

"I think it was probably the first and also the last time he did. Most probably it was a slip of the tongue, a revelation he later regretted, and hoped she wouldn't repeat."

"Did he ever reach out to her?" asked Harriet.

"I don't think he even remembered who she was. It's my impression that Tab slept with a lot of women over the years, another fact that he forgot to mention to his wife."

"I wonder what pushed Madison over the edge," said Harriet.

"You have to remember that on that same morning Madison had heard her husband argue with Saul Goff. She claimed she hadn't overheard the argument but it's safe to say that she had. That's how she discovered that Tab had an affair with Adima Goff. Coming on the heels of that, she finds out that Tab had a vasectomy years ago, before they married and before he made her a lot of promises about starting a family, and at the same time she discovers that he had a one-night stand with Xanthe, which probably wasn't the only one."

"A lot to swallow for a person," Brutus grunted. "This Tab Fitch was something else."

"I wonder what Madame Burnett would make of that man," said Dooley.

"Please, Dooley," said Harriet, holding up a paw. "Don't mention that name ever again!"

"I can still smell it, you know," said Brutus. "That foul stench penetrated all my pores."

"It's just human waste," I said. "All perfectly natural and biodegradable, I'm sure."

"Still. No reason to take a shower in the stuff," Brutus grumbled.

"Let's promise each other here and now never to talk

about the 'incident' again," said Harriet. "Can we all agree on that?"

We all murmured our approval. From now on the incident was closed.

"Why did you say that someone put the hunch in Saul's head to look for the murder weapon in Xanthe and Rasheed's suite?" asked Dooley. "Was that person Madison?"

"She made a throwaway comment to Saul that morning during breakfast," I said. "Reminding him of his own theory that a crazed fan might have killed Tab. It made Saul think, and he quickly decided that Xanthe Bergson was a perfect fit for his theory, especially since the police was already looking at her as a suspect after her arrest."

"Clever," said Brutus, as he started licking himself, then sniffed at his fur and stopped.

We'd all had dinner, and now it was time to relax. So we lay down on the porch swing and would have dozed off if not suddenly loud voices intruded upon our peace and quiet. We opened our eyes to find that our party had been crashed by… Gran and Scarlett!

And they hadn't arrived without bearing gifts. On Scarlett's arm was a man dressed in a captain's uniform, with a neatly trimmed beard and a twinkle in his eyes. And on Gran's arm… was also a man I'd never seen before.

"Surprise!" Gran cried.

There were happy noises as the family welcomed the two ladies back, though I could tell from Tex's face he wasn't all that happy with this surprise. Sometimes a man needs to fly solo—and by flying solo I mean without the presence of his mother-in-law in his life.

"I didn't think you were due back so soon!" said Marge as she hugged her mom.

"I know, but the ship ran into a cliff and sprung a leak," said Gran. "Like the Titanic, but without the loss of life, thank God. Though also without Leo, I'm sorry to say. So we had to bail out early."

"The good news is that they're going to comp us part of our trip," said Scarlett, "which means we get to go on another cruise soon."

"This time hopefully in the actual Caribbean, not Norway."

"And who are these two gentlemen?" asked Odelia.

"This is Rafi Kowarski," said Scarlett. "He was the captain of the ship."

"Pleased to meet you," said Mr. Kowarski as he took a courteous bow and kissed first Odelia's hand, then Marge's hand, before finally kissing Charlene's hand, much to the dismay of—respectively—Chase, Tex and Uncle Alec.

"And this is Dallas de Pravé," said Gran, gesturing to her companion.

He was a stocky sort of man, with skin so tan it was almost orange. I would have pegged him in his early seventies, though he still had a full head of white hair. He also had a broad smile and the kind of square jaw and cleft chin you don't see very often. He reminded me of Cary Grant. He was dressed in a white suit and made a slight bow, then followed Mr. Kowarski's example and started kissing hands right, left and center.

"So who's he?" asked Marge in a whisper.

Gran beamed at her daughter in response, and returned, in a whisper so loud they could probably hear it all the way in Norway, "He's a billionaire. And he's my fiancé!"

THE END

Thanks for reading! If you want to know when a new Nic Saint book comes out, sign up for Nic's mailing list: nicsaint.com/news

EXCERPT FROM PURRFECT BABY (MAX 49)

Chapter One

Dotty Berg relaxed in front of the vanity mirror and started removing her makeup. She wasn't usually the kind of girl who liked to use excessive makeup but in her line of work it was unfortunately a given that she should. In spite of the fact that tonight had been a success she felt bone-tired. Calista would be pleased—the client perhaps less so, even though she'd gotten them the results they paid for. But that wasn't her fault now was it?

She mechanically removed the last remnants of eyeliner from her eyes and for a moment gazed at her reflection in the mirror. A remarkably fresh-faced young woman stared back at her. Remarkable because she'd done this job for so long now she had become a little world-weary. But fortunately that hadn't yet had an effect on her good looks. And nor it should. The moment she started being affected by the turmoil that her chosen profession inevitably brought with it, she'd quit. That's what she had always told Calista and

EXCERPT FROM PURRFECT BABY (MAX 49)

that's how it would be. Then again—the work did pay shockingly well.

She checked her phone for messages and repaired to the bed, prepared to get ready for the night. It had gotten later than she thought, the client requiring a lot of patient handholding and encouragement but finally she'd gotten him exactly where she wanted him. It was a skill set not easily acquired but one she was nevertheless proud of.

And as she stretched out languorously on top of the duvet, she thought she heard a sound from the modest little hallway. Had she forgotten to close the door? It was entirely possible. These last couple of days had been challenging, and sometimes she didn't know where her head was at.

With a tired groan, she sat up and swung her feet from the bed. Hugging her pink satin dressing gown around herself, she shuffled over to have a look. Moments later, she was staggering back into her bedroom, grabbing for her phone. And she'd just started typing a message of distress to Calista when the phone was unceremoniously snatched from her trembling fingers and she was pushed back on the bed. And as he straddled her, she knew that this time she'd gone too far.

Calista Dunne had drifted off to sleep on the couch, a glass of Pinot Noir still in her hand, the TV blaring away and providing the background sound to a pretty sweet dream. In her dream she was relaxing poolside in Mallorca. The sun was warm on her skin, the clear blue water from the pool lapping pleasantly at her feet, the cares of the world a million miles away.

She woke up and automatically grabbed for her phone to see if her husband had left her any messages. He was away on

EXCERPT FROM PURRFECT BABY (MAX 49)

business so she had the house to herself. She yawned until she caught the odd message Dotty had sent. 'He's come back—you've got to—'

"Got to what?" she murmured as she blinked, bleary-eyed, at the message.

She immediately placed the phone to her ear and waited for Dotty to pick up. But Dotty didn't pick up. The special app they used to keep in touch just kept on ringing and ringing to no avail.

She pursed her lips and chewed the inside of her bottom lip, a habit she was trying to break since it could only lead to premature wrinklage.

He's come back. That could mean two things, and in both cases it was probably bad news. Or why else would Dotty feel the need to send her a message at this late hour?

For a few moments she felt irresolute, and she'd already decided to head over there to stave off disaster, when her phone buzzed. It was Dotty again: 'It's fine. He forgot his wallet. Hope I didn't wake you.' Smiley face, smiley face, smiley face, heart emoji.

She smiled and relaxed. False alarm. Still. That self-defense training she'd signed her girls up for was starting to feel like a better idea every day. Maybe even shooting lessons.

She splashed some more of the Pinot into her glass—keep that nice buzz going—and sank back down on the couch.

Moments later, she was fast asleep, and only woke up when he was already straddling her, tying a nylon stocking around her neck and pulling—hard.

Chapter Two

Vesta Muffin didn't often visit the shelter that carried her name, even though she knew she probably should. When her son had opened it along with his girlfriend Charlene Butterwick, the town's mayor, she'd even promised to volunteer there, but that had never materialized of course. In her defense, she was a busy woman, and her time was probably better spent elsewhere. And besides, the Vesta Muffin Animal Shelter had a perfectly capable manager now taking care of things. Marsella Horowicz had been handpicked by Charlene to run the shelter and by all accounts she was doing a great job of it.

The shelter itself still looked new and clean, contrary to the pound that had existed before, and which had been an abomination and a thorn in the side of every animal lover in town. At the new shelter the animals were well taken care of by a small contingent of volunteers who didn't stint in their affection for the creatures who were forced to spend time there, whether short or long, depending how quickly new homes could be found.

Vesta had decided to pay a visit to the shelter with her new boyfriend Dallas de Pravé, a wealthy businessman and investor she'd met on her recent Norwegian cruise. He was Finnish, as far as she knew, and as rich as the sea in those Norwegian fjords was deep. And so if there was anyone who could invest in the shelter it was definitely Dallas.

The billionaire - tan, stocky, handsome and about Vesta's own age - was bobbing his head with distinct interest as Marsella showed them around the facility.

"So how long does it usually take you to find a new home for your darlings?" Vesta wanted to know.

"Days, sometimes. Weeks at the most."

"That's good," said Vesta as she stared at a particularly moody-looking mutt who stared back at her as if to say: 'So what's your problem then, sweetheart?'

Marsella, who was fortyish and very efficient but also very blond and blue-eyed, was standing a little too close to

Dallas to Vesta's liking, so she inserted herself between the two, even as Dallas pointed to a tiny doggie and said, "What he?"

"That's a Brussels Griffon," said Marsella. "Her name is Windex."

"Windex?" asked Vesta with a frown. "What kind of a name is that?"

"It's the name her previous owner gave her."

"What was he? A window washer?"

"No, she was an elderly lady who had to move into a nursing home where unfortunately they don't allow pets. And since her daughter wasn't interested in providing a home for Windex she was forced to put her up with us until we can find her a suitable new pet parent." She gave Vesta a gentle smile. "Want to hold her for a moment?"

"Oh, no," said Vesta, waving a hand. "I know what you're trying to do, and you have to cut that out right now. My home is full. Four cats is more than enough for any person."

"Win-dex," Dallas murmured, enunciating carefully. "Win… dex."

"You can take her, if you want," said Vesta. "You like dogs? Dallas?"

"Mh?" said the aged billionaire.

"Do you like dogs?" she repeated, gesticulating extensively.

"Yes, yes," he murmured with a smile. "Windex dog."

"He doesn't speak English?" asked Marsella.

"He's Finnish," Vesta explained.

"How did you meet?"

"Aboard a cruise ship in Norway. I told him my name was Vesta Muffin and he said 'I like American muffin' and we never looked back. So how long has Windex been here?"

"Three weeks, and she's really pining, I can tell. It's heartbreaking, really."

EXCERPT FROM PURRFECT BABY (MAX 49)

"It is," Vesta agreed as she took in the poor little creature that was staring at her with its liquid brown eyes, as if imploring her to do something. "Why is no one taking her?"

"I don't know. She looks a little funny, so kids tend not to like her and adults think she's probably too set in her ways after having spent so many years with the same person. I try to tell them she's the sweetest thing on earth but they just look at her and shiver."

Vesta frowned. "Why? She looks fine to me."

Marsella dropped her voice and whispered into Vesta's ear, "They say she looks like a bat."

Vesta studied the tiny doggie some more. Windex did look a little like a bat, with her big ears and her small snout. Even the coloring was a little bat-like. "So?" she said. "Kids love those Batman movies. You could tell them Windex is Batman's little helper."

Marsella laughed. "Now there's an idea."

"Win-dex," Dallas said slowly. "Dog." He smiled. "Windex, dog."

"Yes, yes, Windex is a dog," said Vesta impatiently. The man might be made of money but he was definitely an odd bird. "Okay, fine," she said, making one of her trademark swift decisions. "I'll take her. Did she get all her shots and stuff?"

Marsella stared at her. "You'll take her?"

"Sure, why not? She looks like a sweet little thing, and my grandson-in-law loves dogs."

"Absolutely," said Marsella, and pressed a warm hand upon Vesta's arm. "You won't be sorry."

"I'm not so sure about that," Vesta murmured as she followed Marsella to the office.

Behind them, Dallas trailed. "Windex dog," he was muttering.

In the office she met one of the volunteers: Shelley Eccleston looked like a teenager but was probably older than she looked. Then again, all young people looked like teenagers to Vesta, with their unblemished faces and their peach-perfect skin.

"Can you prepare the paperwork for Windex, Shelley?" asked Marsella. "Vesta is taking her home."

"Ooh, that's great!" said the girl with all the fervor of youth. "You're a saint, Mrs. Muffin. An absolute saint."

"Yeah, yeah, yeah," said Vesta as she watched Dallas stare at Shelley, open-mouthed as if he'd never seen a pretty girl before. "Better close that trap or you'll catch flies," she told him, but of course he didn't understand a word she said. She was starting to regret bringing this particular billionaire home with her. Tough to communicate if he only spoke Finnish—or at least that's what she assumed those garbled guttural tones that sometimes fell from his tongue when he talked into his phone were—and she only spoke English.

She'd hoped the language of love would see them through but there had been none of that either. At first she'd thought he was simply shy, but now she was starting to think he was one of those eunuchs. Or was it unicorns? She never knew which was which.

At least he wasn't married—or at least she didn't think he was. No mention of a Mrs. Dallas de Pravé had ever been made, and when she googled the guy she hadn't found any evidence of a marital entanglement either. Like her, he was widowed with two kids, both now already with kids themselves. All of them had funny names like Jarmo and Eeto and Arvo and reportedly the de Pravés were amongst the richest families in Finland.

A young kid walked in, looking as youthful and fresh-faced as Shelley, and the latter said, "Can you get Windex ready, Gavin? Mrs. Muffin is taking her home with her."

EXCERPT FROM PURRFECT BABY (MAX 49)

The kid stared at her. "Mrs. Muffin?" he said finally. "Vesta Muffin?"

"That's my name—don't wear it out," she quipped.

The kid's eyes swiveled from her to the picture of her that hung next to the 'Vesta Muffin Animal Shelter' sign behind the counter and he blinked, then a smile spread across his freckled face. "It's an honor, Mrs. Muffin. You did a great thing starting this shelter."

She would have told the kid who was probably all of nineteen that she hadn't exactly started the shelter, merely given her name to it, but who was she to deprive this young man of this honest pleasure. "I feel it's important we all do what we can to give our furry little friends a better life... Gavin, is it?"

He nodded fervently. "Gavin Blemish. And you're absolutely right, Mrs. Muffin."

"Blemish, as in Garwen Blemish?"

"Yeah, he's my dad."

"I always buy my shoes there. Great place."

"Best place in town," he said, and flashed her a toothy smile. Perfect white teeth, of course, she couldn't help but notice with a small measure of chagrin. "Next time you come in I'll make sure you get a discount, Mrs. Muffin."

"Oh, so you work there, do you?"

"Yeah, I'm only volunteering here," he said with a slight diminution of happiness. "Though I'd love to work here full-time," he added, eyeing her with a look of hope as if she was made of money and he wouldn't mind having some. "I absolutely adore our animals."

"Uh-huh. More than shoes, you mean?"

"Oh, absolutely. I mean, shoes are fine, but animals—well, they need us, don't they?"

"Same here," said Shelley.

"So where do you work, Shelley?" asked Vesta, who

wondered if these two were boyfriend and girlfriend. They looked as if they might be.

"I work for my dad, actually. He runs Eccleston Concrete. It's a cement factory," she explained. "I work in the office. But I spend as much time here at your shelter as I can."

She would have dissuaded them from the notion that she actually owned the shelter but they were both gazing at her with such abject admiration that she didn't have the heart. "Well, you're both doing a great job here," she said. "And I can only thank you and tell you to keep up the good work."

She glanced over to Dallas, who was now eyeing a chart that offered an overview of the different species of dogs that are out there, and was mouthing their names to himself. If she ever managed to talk to the guy, and convince him to invest in the shelter, maybe Marsella could offer both Shelley and Gavin an actual contract.

Then again, who was she kidding? She'd seen the numbers. There simply wasn't enough work for three full-timers. So she merely smiled encouragingly at the two young people and watched them return to work—getting little Windex ready for his new home.

Chapter Three

Once Vesta and her companion had left, the warm sensation of accomplishment that had briefly swept through Marsella quickly dissipated, and the cloud of dread that had been hanging over her all week made a sudden comeback, like it always did. Gavin had gone to clean out the gerbil cages and now it was just Marsella and Shelley.

Shelley must have noticed something, for she suddenly said, "Is everything all right?"

She could have lied and told her everything was fine, but Shelley was no fool. Plus, in the months they'd known each

EXCERPT FROM PURRFECT BABY (MAX 49)

other they'd become great friends. Which was odd, since she could have been Shelley's mom, but Shelley was such a warmhearted person and so easy to talk to it wasn't hard to see why she'd become increasingly fond of the young woman.

She finally sighed and slumped against the counter. "It's Dewey. Yet another one of his old girlfriends came crawling out of the woodwork last week to warn me about him."

"Not again," said Shelley, her expression a vivid tableau of compassion.

Marsella nodded. "On Facebook this time. Sent me a friend request and a message out of the blue. Said she'd heard about the wedding and wanted me to know what kind of a man Dewey Toneu really is. Then if I still wanted to marry him at least I'd know what I was letting myself in for."

"Did you tell Dewey?"

She shook her head. "Not yet."

"How long ago was the affair?"

"Um, about... three years ago maybe? Apparently he was juggling five different girlfriends at the time, and they all accidentally found out about each other when Dewey sent a group email to all of them and forgot to put them in BCC. They actually got together one night and discovered he'd promised all of them he'd marry them. Or so she says, this Mary-Lynn." She was trying hard to keep the bitterness and anxiousness out of her voice but judging from the look on Shelley's face she wasn't doing a particularly good job.

"You have to talk to Dewey, Marsella."

"I did talk to him, when the first of his exes got in touch. He admitted dating her, but said that he'd been a different person back then." She gave Shelley a hesitant look. "He says that none of those girls meant anything to him. That I'm the only one for him now. *The* one. That the moment we met he knew his old life of casual dating was finally over."

"He could be right. Three years is a long time. He's probably older and wiser now."

"You think?"

"Has any of these girls dated him since you met?"

"No. Mary-Lynn was three years ago, and the other one, um... Francine—four years."

"See? I'm sure that if Dewey was cheating on you, you'd know. It's hard to keep this stuff secret in this day and age of social media."

"Yeah, but if he really was dating some other girl she wouldn't tell me, would she? She'd simply hope the wedding doesn't go through. Or maybe she's one of those girls who don't mind dating a married man—even prefers it, for the lack of attachment."

"Look, if you really wanted to be sure, you'd almost have to hire a private detective. Have Dewey followed around the clock to see if he's as committed to you as he says he is."

She gave the girl a keen look.

"Oh, no, you didn't," said Shelley, clearly shocked.

"No, I didn't," she admitted. "But I have considered it."

"Well, maybe you should. Just to put your mind at ease."

"It's just that... he's such a catch, you know. It's very hard to date a man who's as attractive and as successful as Dewey. A lot of insecurities suddenly start to pop up."

"Hey, don't sell yourself short, Marsella," said Shelley, giving her a gentle nudge. "You're quite a catch yourself, you know. In fact it's Dewey who should be worried, not you."

She smiled and felt her mood lift. "You always know what to say to make me feel better, don't you?"

"Then it's a good thing you made me your maid of honor."

Just then, a family with two little girls walked into the office, and work beckoned, cutting their conversation short. But as she escorted the family out to take a look at the kennels, she found herself revisiting the idea of hiring a private detective. If it offered her peace of mind, why not? And so she decided to check listings for PIs in the area tonight.

Chapter Four

It had been a particularly lazy morning for us. Odelia and Chase had both left and gone to work, and for once all four of us had opted to stay home and relax instead. Lately Odelia hadn't stepped out of the office much, since she was about to give birth any moment now, and so Dan had figured it was unwise for her to go out and interview people until after she'd delivered the baby. Odelia's opinion in the matter was different, of course: she wanted to keep busy right up until the last possible moment, and her doctor hadn't given her any indication why she couldn't, which strengthened her in her view.

But with nothing much going on at the paper, and nothing going on at the police station, Dooley, Brutus, Harriet and myself had figured we should take advantage of these final days or weeks before the big change was upon us: the arrival of the new baby.

"So do you think it's going to be a boy or a girl?" asked Dooley, not for the first time.

"I don't know, Dooley, and Odelia isn't telling, so speculation is pointless."

"But why, Max? Why aren't they telling us? We have a right to know."

"Not really," I said. "And besides, maybe they don't know themselves."

"I think they know," said Harriet. "And they're simply not telling anyone."

"But why!" Dooley insisted. "We have to know, so we can prepare ourselves."

"What difference does it make?" I said. "Babies are babies, whatever their gender."

"That's where you're wrong, Max," said Brutus. "There's a huge difference."

"Of course there is," I said, yawning and hoping everyone would shut up so I could get some nap time in. Why else had we stayed home if not to enjoy some peace and quiet while we still could?

"Boys are much more rambunctious," said Brutus. "Girls are quieter. So my vote is for a girl."

"It's not an election, sweetie," said Harriet. "We don't get to vote."

"I know, but if we could vote, I'd choose a girl. So fingers crossed."

"You don't even have fingers," I pointed out.

"I think it's going to be a girl," said Dooley.

"What makes you say that?" said Brutus.

"One of your silly documentaries again?" said Harriet.

"They're not silly, and for your information I read about this on the internet. You can see from the shape of the belly whether it's going to be a boy or a girl, and I'm almost one hundred percent sure Odelia's belly is a girl belly. It's more... oval? More round, you know."

I didn't know, and frankly I didn't care. Babies are pretty much all the same in my experience: small and loud and annoying. I just hoped they'd get it over with and bring it home already. And if it did prove to be too much for us, we could always move next door and spend the formative years of the child's life with Marge and Tex.

"How long does it take for a baby to become less of a nuisance?" I asked.

"Years," said Brutus.

"Years?" It wasn't the answer I'd hoped for. "I thought months."

EXCERPT FROM PURRFECT BABY (MAX 49)

"Oh, no. They only develop into actual human beings when they get their first job and strike out on their own, which is probably when they turn twenty-four, maybe twenty-three if you're lucky. If they can't land a decent job they can't move into their own place and then you're stuck with them pretty much indefinitely. In fact Tigger was telling us the other day that his human's daughter is still living with them, even though she's thirty."

"Thirty!"

"Can you imagine?"

"Thirty years of diapers," said Dooley knowingly.

"I don't think kids wear diapers until they're thirty," said Harriet. "Probably they grow out of the habit much sooner."

"Some kids are fine," said Brutus. "Tigger's human's daughter is all right and she has been all right for a long time. Doesn't scream or shout or make his life miserable. In fact she's the one who feeds him now and even cleans out his litter box. But they tell me that's rare. Most kids refuse to do anything around the home. They just sort of mope around."

We all looked appropriately impressed. "Tigger is lucky," I said finally.

"It's a lottery," said Brutus, repeating a universal truth we'd heard from many sources. "Either you end up with some pocket psychopath who likes to pull tails and poke eyes, or you end up with Tigger's human's daughter, who's a very normal, very nice person."

"Which is why we need to pray Odelia has a girl, you guys," said Dooley. "Because we all know that girls are nice and boys are hellraisers who'll make our lives miserable."

And as the discussion raged on, I decided to tune them all out and catch up on my nap time. Whether Odelia had a girl or a boy, at least that way I was way ahead of the curve.

Just then, the sliding glass door slid back and Gran walked in. That strange billionaire fiancé she's been hanging out with lately wasn't with her this time. The man hadn't exchanged one intelligible word with any of the rest of the family, and all he seemed to do was follow Gran around everywhere, a sort of perpetual smile on his face. He seemed nice enough, but it would be even nicer if he decided to give us the benefit of his conversation.

"Where is everyone?" asked Gran.

"Work," I said as I adjusted my position on the couch.

And that's when I saw it.

A dog. In Gran's arms.

"What's that, Gran?" asked Dooley, who'd noticed the same curious phenomenon.

"What do you think it is? A dog, of course. Okay, so I'm just going to leave her here," she said, and deposited the small bundle of fur on the couch right next to us!

"Gran, what are you doing!" Harriet cried as she jumped up from her position.

"Oh, don't get your knickers in a twist," said Gran irritably. "It's just a dog."

"But... whose dog is it?" asked Brutus, eyeing the creature suspiciously.

"Chase's dog, of course. Though he doesn't know it yet."

"Chase's dog!" Brutus cried. "But Chase already has a pet. Me!"

"Well, so now he's got another one. And besides, Chase always wanted a dog."

"But Gran!" Harriet practically wailed.

Gran held up her hand. "No need to thank me. You're welcome."

And with these words, she strode out again. Then, as if she'd just remembered, she opened the door a crack and said, "Oh, her name is Windex, by the way." And was gone.

ABOUT NIC

Nic has a background in political science and before being struck by the writing bug worked odd jobs around the world (including but not limited to massage therapist in Mexico, gardener in Italy, restaurant manager in India, and Berlitz teacher in Belgium).

When he's not writing he enjoys curling up with a good (comic) book, watching British crime dramas, French comedies or Nancy Meyers movies, sampling pastry (apple cake!), pasta and chocolate (preferably the dark variety), twisting himself into a pretzel doing morning yoga, going for a run, and spoiling his big red tomcat Tommy.

He lives with his wife (and aforementioned cat) in a small village smack dab in the middle of absolutely nowhere and is probably writing his next 'Mysteries of Max' book right now.

www.nicsaint.com

ALSO BY NIC SAINT

The Mysteries of Max
Purrfect Murder
Purrfectly Deadly
Purrfect Revenge
Purrfect Heat
Purrfect Crime
Purrfect Rivalry
Purrfect Peril
Purrfect Secret
Purrfect Alibi
Purrfect Obsession
Purrfect Betrayal
Purrfectly Clueless
Purrfectly Royal
Purrfect Cut
Purrfect Trap
Purrfectly Hidden
Purrfect Kill
Purrfect Boy Toy
Purrfectly Dogged
Purrfectly Dead
Purrfect Saint
Purrfect Advice
Purrfect Passion

A Purrfect Gnomeful
Purrfect Cover
Purrfect Patsy
Purrfect Son
Purrfect Fool
Purrfect Fitness
Purrfect Setup
Purrfect Sidekick
Purrfect Deceit
Purrfect Ruse
Purrfect Swing
Purrfect Cruise
Purrfect Harmony
Purrfect Sparkle
Purrfect Cure
Purrfect Cheat
Purrfect Catch
Purrfect Design
Purrfect Life
Purrfect Thief
Purrfect Crust
Purrfect Bachelor
Purrfect Double
Purrfect Date
Purrfect Hit
Purrfect Baby

The Mysteries of Max Box Sets

Box Set 1 (Books 1-3)

Box Set 2 (Books 4-6)
Box Set 3 (Books 7-9)
Box Set 4 (Books 10-12)
Box Set 5 (Books 13-15)
Box Set 6 (Books 16-18)
Box Set 7 (Books 19-21)
Box Set 8 (Books 22-24)
Box Set 9 (Books 25-27)
Box Set 10 (Books 28-30)
Box Set 11 (Books 31-33)
Box Set 12 (Books 34-36)
Box Set 13 (Books 37-39)
Box Set 14 (Books 40-42)
Box Set 15 (Books 43-45)

The Mysteries of Max Big Box Sets

Big Box Set 1 (Books 1-10)
Big Box Set 2 (Books 11-20)

The Mysteries of Max Shorts

Purrfect Santa (3 shorts in one)
Purrfectly Flealess
Purrfect Wedding

Nora Steel

Murder Retreat

The Kellys

Murder Motel
Death in Suburbia

Emily Stone
Murder at the Art Class

Washington & Jefferson
First Shot

Alice Whitehouse
Spooky Times
Spooky Trills
Spooky End
Spooky Spells

Ghosts of London
Between a Ghost and a Spooky Place
Public Ghost Number One
Ghost Save the Queen
Box Set 1 (Books 1-3)
A Tale of Two Harrys
Ghost of Girlband Past
Ghostlier Things

Charleneland
Deadly Ride
Final Ride

Neighborhood Witch Committee
Witchy Start
Witchy Worries
Witchy Wishes

Saffron Diffley

Crime and Retribution

Vice and Verdict

Felonies and Penalties (Saffron Diffley Short 1)

The B-Team

Once Upon a Spy

Tate-à-Tate

Enemy of the Tates

Ghosts vs. Spies

The Ghost Who Came in from the Cold

Witchy Fingers

Witchy Trouble

Witchy Hexations

Witchy Possessions

Witchy Riches

Box Set 1 (Books 1-4)

The Mysteries of Bell & Whitehouse

One Spoonful of Trouble

Two Scoops of Murder

Three Shots of Disaster

Box Set 1 (Books 1-3)

A Twist of Wraith

A Touch of Ghost

A Clash of Spooks

Box Set 2 (Books 4-6)

The Stuffing of Nightmares

A Breath of Dead Air

An Act of Hodd

Box Set 3 (Books 7-9)

A Game of Dons

Standalone Novels

When in Bruges

The Whiskered Spy

ThrillFix

Homejacking

The Eighth Billionaire

The Wrong Woman

Printed in Great Britain
by Amazon